Cast of

Aloysius P. Graham. Everyone, ~~~~~~~~~~~~~~~ ...~~-loving "Wishy," whose salty language wo~~~~ impress a sailor. Because he sold their house for a good profit, he and his daughter are homeless.

Virginia Graham. His daughter and an ex-Marine, she isn't averse to hooking up with a man, so long as it's on her terms.

Jim Larson. The younger of the town's two doctors, he's wooing Virginia in spite of the Larson-Graham family feud.

Maude Watson. A 50-year-old widow, she's trying to keep the mansion's roof over her head and the police from discovering the family's dark secret. She likes her martinis—and her men—strong.

Una Randall. Maude's spoiled younger sister. She's willing to marry anyone, from the doctor to the butler, to escape her present poverty.

Ed Randall. Una's ex, he's bunking at the mansion at Maude's invitation. He wouldn't mind remarrying Una.

Bertram (Bert) Hanson. The older of the town's two doctors. It isn't true that he still has the first dime he ever made but he's got at least seven cents of it left. He'd like to marry either Una or Maude.

Susan Falks. Hanson's nurse. Gus is the love of her life. Of course, if Gus isn't around . . .

Wister. Maude and Una's butler, he works a second job to help out. He'd like to be more than a servant to Una. He certainly has more money than she does.

P.X. Smith. He's an elderly visiting businessman with a black goatee who bears an uncanny resemblance to Maude and Una's father.

Alex Viter. He's an amateur detective and a friend of Ed's, who agrees to do a little snooping. He especially likes to snoop in Maude's vicinity.

The Andersons. Bert's servants. He resents the fact that they have a better social life than he does.

Books by Constance & Gwenyth Little

The Grey Mist Murders (1938)*
Black-Headed Pins (1938)*
The Black Gloves (1939)*
Black Corridors (1940)*
The Black Paw (1941)*
The Black Shrouds (1941)*
The Black Thumb (1942)*
The Black Rustle (1943)*
The Black Honeymoon (1944)*
Great Black Kanba (1944)*
The Black Eye (1945)*
The Black Stocking (1946)*
The Black Goatee (1947)*
The Black Coat (1948)*
The Black Piano (1948)
The Black Smith (1950)
The Black House (1950)
The Blackout (1951)
The Black Dream (1952)
The Black Curl (1953)
The Black Iris (1953)

*reprinted by the Rue Morgue Press
as of January 2004

The Black Goatee

by Constance & Gwenyth Little

The Rue Morgue Press
Boulder / Lyons

Printed at Johnson Printing
Boulder, Colorado

The Rue Morgue Press
P.O. Box 4119
Boulder, CO 80306

PRINTED IN THE UNITED STATES OF AMERICA

About the Littles

Although all but one of their books had "black" in the title, the 21 mysteries of Constance (1899-1980) and Gwenyth (1903-1985) Little were far from somber affairs. The two Australian-born sisters from East Orange, New Jersey, were far more interested in coaxing chuckles than in inducing chills from their readers.

Indeed, after their first book, *The Grey Mist Murders*, appeared in 1938, Constance rebuked an interviewer for suggesting that their murders weren't realistic by saying, "Our murderers strangle. We have no sliced-up corpses in our books." However, as the books mounted, the Littles did go in for all sorts of gruesome murder methods—"horrible," was the way their own mother described them—which included the occasional sliced-up corpse.

But the murders were always off stage and tempered by comic scenes in which bodies and other objects, including swimming pools, were constantly disappearing and reappearing. The action took place in large old mansions, boarding houses, hospitals, hotels, or on trains or ocean liners, anywhere the Littles could gather together a large cast of eccentric characters, many of whom seemed to have escaped from a Kaufman play or a Capra movie. The typical Little heroine—each book was a stand-alone—often fell under suspicion herself and turned detective to keep the police from slapping the cuffs on. Whether she was a working woman or a spoiled little rich brat, she always spoke her mind, kept her rather sarcastic sense of humor, and got her man, both murderer and husband. But if marriage was in the offing, it was always on her terms and the vows were taken with more than a touch of cynicism. Love was grand, but it was even grander if the husband could either pitch in with the cooking and cleaning or was wealthy enough to hire household help.

The Littles wrote all their books in bed—"Chairs give one backaches," Gwenyth complained—with Constance providing detailed plot outlines while Gwenyth did the final drafts. Over the years that pattern changed somewhat, but Constance always insisted that Gwen "not mess up my clues." Those clues were everywhere, and the Littles made sure there were no loose ends. Seemingly irrelevant events were revealed to be of major significance in the final summation. The plots were often preposterous, a fact often recognized by both the Littles and their characters, all of whom seem to be winking at the reader, almost as if sharing a private joke. You just have to accept the fact that there are different natural laws in the wacky universe created by these sisters. There are no other mystery writers quite like them. At times, their books seem to be an odd collaboration between P.G. Wodehouse and Cornell Woolrich.

The Littles published their two final novels, *The Black Curl* and *The Black Iris*, in 1953, and if they missed writing after that, they were at least able to devote more time to their real passion—traveling. The two made at least three trips around the world at a time when that would have been a major undertaking. For more information on the Littles and their books, see the introductions by Tom & Enid Schantz to The Rue Morgue Press editions of *The Black Gloves* and *The Black Honeymoon*.

CHAPTER 1

IT WAS A LARGE house, low and long, with white columns rising against a background of red brick at the middle section and ample wings extending along each side. There was an impressive white door with a brass knocker, and a formally banked mass of rhododendrons at each side. An imposing place, and yet it had an indefinable air of incipient neglect. It seemed, somehow, that in another year the rhododendrons would be straggling and the knocker tarnished.

Aloysius P. Graham mounted two brick steps and scowled at the white door. All those rooms, and most of them empty, with only the two women and that phony butler living here. Terrific postwar housing shortage, and did they rise up and show their patriotism by renting out the two wings? They did not, and nothing he could say would make them see reason. Well, he intended to go in and try again, and that would make three times this week. Perhaps if he pounded at them often enough, they'd break down.

He ignored the discreet electric bell and banged savagely with the brass knocker, because it relieved his feelings, and presently Wister swung back the door, blinking and peering inquiringly. His face fell when he saw that it was merely A.P. Graham, and he said with a touch of austerity, "I don't believe they will see you, sir. They told me, last time—"

Aloysius brushed him aside and walked into the wide, cool hall.

"That's all right, Wister. They're afraid I'm going to try to get them to rent me a room again, but as a matter of fact, this is purely a social call. Where are they?"

"I don't know," Wister said indifferently. He had removed his coat and was carefully hanging it in the hall closet. "They're around somewhere." He walked back to the end of the hall, made his way through the kitchen, and entered his own small bedroom, where he lay down upon the bed and appeared to go to sleep immediately.

Aloysius, who had followed him, stood regarding him with a good deal of bitterness, which was considerably heightened by the fact that the comfortable little bedroom had an adjoining bathroom—small, too, but gleaming with tile and modern plumbing.

"That lug!" Aloysius thought furiously. "A room and bath to himself, and what do I have?" He turned away, stamped back into the entrance hall, and yelled, "Maude! Una! Where are you?"

There was no answer from his two cousins and no sound, and he presently began an angry search through the lower rooms which eventually brought him to the right wing of the house. This was maintained as a sort of museum and was cluttered untidily with antiques, paintings, and various useless but supposedly ornamental objects that had been collected from all over the world. The place was dusty and disorderly, and there were several white squares on the walls where pictures had been removed.

Aloysius was conscious of a sort of superior disapproval. Their father had always kept the house in spotless order, and now look at it. What was the matter with the girls, anyway? They had enough to keep the place up. The old man had left them a pile.

He returned, frowning, to the main part of the house. They were lazy and sloppy, that was all. And where were they, anyhow? It was almost lunch time. He called again into the silence and wondered suddenly if they were hiding somewhere, waiting for him to go.

Well, he wasn't going, and they'd have to come out sometime. He wandered over to the piano, sat down, and played a few ditties, but that didn't work, so he presently got up again and went across the hall to the door that opened into the left wing.

It was locked, as usual. They always kept it locked. Said it was where their father had lived, and they wanted it kept just the way he had left it. A shrine.

Aloysius made a noise of utter contempt. They simply couldn't be

bothered sorting out the old man's things, cleaning the wing and setting it to rights, that was all. They were getting pretty damned close
with their money these days. Servants were hard to get, of course,
but they were even doing the gardening themselves. Gardening!
He whistled softly, That's where they were, working outside in the
garden.

He went out through the library to the back terrace and saw them
almost at once. They were some distance away, working over some
vines that might have been sweet or utilitarian pea. He drew in a breath
to shout and then changed his mind. They mightn't like it; better walk
down to them instead. He walked along to the end of the terrace,
glancing idly at the windows as he passed. The last one was almost
opaque with dust and dirt, and he realized that it was in the left wing.
He stepped over and, shading his eyes, tried to see inside, but he
could not make out much beyond a section of dimly lighted hallway,
the floor gray with dust.

They were letting the place go to rack and ruin, Aloysius thought
irritably. It was nothing to do with him, of course, although he was
their nearest relative

The train of his thoughts was abruptly broken. He had absentmindedly pushed at the window, and it responded by sliding up quite
easily. He gave one quick glance over his shoulder, scrambled in
through the window, and hastily shut it behind him.

He felt a surge of pleasure and interest. Now he could investigate
this mysterious left wing and take his time doing it, too. He had long
wanted to look through this retreat where his uncle Oliver P. Graham
had established himself in comfort and comparative privacy, and where
his spirit no doubt still swanked around and enjoyed itself. Well, if he
ran into it, he'd take it by the seat of the pants and put it out. This set
him to laughing quietly, until the narrow, dusty hall led him to a large
room, where he came face to face with a life-size portrait of Oliver P.
Graham and was instantly sobered. The eyes looked straight down at
him from over the mantel, grim, accusing, and as cold and fishlike as
two oysters.

Aloysius averted his own eyes and looked the room over. It was
luxuriously furnished as a living room, and across one corner there
was a small built-in bar. He went over to peer behind it and felt excite-

ment rising queerly in him. Behind the bar there was a sink, a two-burner electric grill, and a small electric refrigerator.

"A kitchen!" Aloysius whispered shakily. "All the makings for an honest-to-God kitchen!"

He heard the voices of his cousins approaching and froze for an instant before he crept back through the hall and peered cautiously out of the dirty window. They had left the vines and were much closer to the house but had stopped to pick some pansies. He watched them for a moment and then walked quietly back to Oliver's living room with its invaluable little bar.

His inspection took on the air now of a prospective client, and he sneered a little and muttered that he'd like to see upstairs. He found the stairs at the other end of the little hall and mounted to a corresponding hall on the second floor. Three bedrooms opened from it, all nicely furnished, one with twin beds and the other two with comfortable-looking double beds. There was also a bathroom, aggressively tiled and outfitted in pale lavender and deep violet. The facilities, in deep violet porcelain and plastic, seemed vaguely indecent to Aloysius, and he turned away and after a moment's hesitation mounted a narrow flight of stairs to an attic.

He found broken and discarded furniture, dusty trunks, old magazines and books, and suddenly, from amongst this ordinary, magpie collection, he saw, again, the portrait of Oliver P. Graham. The eyes, cold, accusing, and grim as ever, looked straight into his.

CHAPTER 2

ALOYSIUS RETREATED in haste that bordered on panic. On the second floor he paused to wipe his forehead shakily with his handkerchief, and he wondered, confusedly, how the portrait could have got up to the attic while he was looking at the bedrooms. He went down to the living room and peered fearfully around the edge of the door and was considerably relieved to find the fishlike eyes still staring down from over the mantel.

So there were two of those portraits. The old goat always was a stickler for having carbon copies made of everything, Aloysius thought, and laughed quietly.

He did not waste any more time, but moved across the room to where French doors looked out onto a terrace at the far end. The doors were locked and bolted at top and bottom, but the key was there. He opened them up, stepped outside, and locked them behind him. He paused, then, and cautiously looked around him.

The terrace was completely secluded from the rest of the garden and extended almost into the woods, where he could see a narrow path. That path, he thought, must lead out onto Main Street, and probably Oliver P. had used it when he wanted a private night out.

Aloysius sighed gustily and with utter content. The setup was perfect, and he wondered why he had not thought of it before. Instead of crawling on his knees to Maude and Una, he'd simply move in, and they'd never know.

Well, no use wasting time. There were things to be done, and he was in a hurry. There was a white picket fence at the edge of the woods, and he was somewhat aggrieved to discover that it ran in an unbroken line, without a gate, so that it was necessary to climb over it in order to gain the path. It seemed the only drawback to an otherwise perfect situation. He felt a spasm of annoyance at Oliver P. for not having done something about it. It was not everyone who could vault a picket fence with ease. Probably he had thought he was fooling his family into believing that he stayed at home every night, and yet there was the pathway through the woods, beyond the fence, for all to see. And who would have cared, anyway? The girls got about, and as for the wife—Aloysius grinned to himself. The whole family had had fun, and no questions asked.

Aloysius vaulted the fence, walked the path through the woods to Main Street, and then broke into a run, after a glance at his watch.

He reached the Kuntree Koffee Shoppe after a smart trot, but was too winded even to greet the slim young figure in gray and raspberry linen who stood there waiting for him.

Her gray eyes lit up with sharp annoyance when she saw him, and she shook back the straight, silky, ash-blonde hair that framed her face.

"This is the last time I'm going to have lunch with you, Father. I simply haven't the time to waste hanging around waiting for you."

He could only pant, but he pushed her inside and steered her to a table. After they had been seated for a moment, he muttered, "Wait— you just wait until I tell you what I've accomplished this morning."

She gave him an exasperated glance and picked up the menu.

Aloysius let her study it for a while and then took a deep breath and exploded his bomb.

"I have an apartment for us."

The girl dropped the menu and strangled over an exclamation of delight, but throughout the subsequent fit of coughing she kept her eyes expectantly on Aloysius, who beamed back at her.

"Oh, Father! That's simply wonderful! Where is it? How many rooms? What is it like?"

This, as Aloysius had known from the beginning, was the really sticky part of the whole thing. He discovered that he was nervous. He tried, nonchalantly, to cross his legs under the table, found that they wouldn't fit, after tilting it and upsetting a glass of water, and murmured, "Er . . ."

Virginia righted the glass and mopped at the water with a napkin, without being wholly conscious of what she was doing.

"Father, tell me! How did you get it? I want to hear all about it."

Aloysius drummed on the table with his fingers and smiled, and she suddenly dropped the napkin, narrowed her eyes at him, and asked suspiciously, "How much is the rent? Not one of these three-hundred-and-seventy-five-a-month touches, is it?"

"No, no," Aloysius said hastily. "No trouble that way. None at all."

"How much?" she asked implacably.

"Nothing."

"What do you mean?"

Aloysius straightened his tie and cleared his throat. "Listen, baby. You know that left wing in Maude's and Una's house? Where old man Graham used to live, and where his spirit still dwells? I got in there today, without anyone knowing—and it's a perfect setup for us. Nothing to stop us moving right in alongside old Ollie's ghost."

Virginia slumped back into her chair and, from the depths of her disappointment, said some very unkind things to her parent. But

Aloysius held his ground and defended his position. He described the bar, which provided kitchen facilities, the terrace where they could sit of an evening, and the violet-colored bathtub into which they could draw hot water from Maude's and Una's boiler. Rather a heartening thought, when he remembered how they had refused him even so much as an attic room.

"Oh, shut up, Father," Virginia said crossly. "We'd no sooner get in there than Maude or Una would discover us, and there'd be a frightful row and we'd be thrown out. If we move from Aunt Elsie's sun parlor, we'll never get it back, and what are we going to do then?"

"Ah, show a little enterprise," Aloysius said largely. "We can always go to the firehouse. I have an in there."

Virginia murmured, "Look who's coming," and Aloysius glanced over his shoulder.

A tall, tanned, blue-eyed man was approaching their table, and Aloysius scowled darkly. "Damned young hound!" he muttered to no one in particular.

The newcomer pulled out a chair and sat down between them.

"Don't mind if I join you?" he asked cheerfully.

Virginia gave him a delicate half-smile, and Aloysius said, "Not at all," and tried to make it obvious that he lied.

Dr. James Larson picked up the menu and asked with unabashed good humor, "What is good today?"

Aloysius glanced at him, and sudden malice gleamed from his eyes.

"I'll tell you one thing that's good for Virginia and me. I've located an apartment."

Dr. Larson dropped the menu and gave him a calculating stare, and then turned to Virginia for possible confirmation.

She found herself quite unable to explain that it was merely another of her father's harebrained schemes, so that after a barely perceptible moment of hesitation she smiled and nodded.

"Where is it?"

"Now don't get excited, Jimmy," Aloysius said loftily. "We can't tell you where it is. The whole thing's a secret, because these people don't want it to get out that they're renting."

"Don't be absurd. How can you keep a thing like that secret?"

"Absurd I may be," Aloysius said furiously, "but we're keeping this secret. It's well worth it, too. Beautiful place—four rooms, storage space, terrace—"

"In that case," Dr. Larson interrupted, "you can rent me one of the rooms. You know how desperate I am, sleeping in my office."

"Sorry," said Aloysius, making it clear that he was not. "We need all the rooms for our own use."

"But you could let me have the storage space," Dr. Larson protested.

Aloysius smiled happily and repeated, "Sorry. We need that for storage."

Dr. Larson turned a pair of outraged blue eyes on Virginia, who raised her shoulders and dropped them again. "I can't see why you're so badly off in your office. It's comfortable enough, and you have everything you need."

"It's lousy," said Dr. Larson simply, "to have to live where you also do your work. After you've been listening to a procession of people with a bellyache, or something, you like to get away from it all." He paused for a moment, looking into space, and then turned suddenly to Aloysius. "By the way, what's the matter with your cousin Una? I've been wanting to talk to you about her, because you're her only relative around here, except Maude, and Maude won't take it seriously. Una is obsessed with fear about something."

CHAPTER 3

VIRGINIA LAUGHED. "Don't let that bother you. Una's afraid of Father. He's been hounding them to rent us part of their house. It's exactly typical of Father—sells our house at an enormous price right over my head, and then proposes to squander the money while Maude and Una harbor us."

"I don't know what you mean by 'harbor us,'" Aloysius said indignantly. "I have offered to pay them board from the first. But anyway, let them go on selfishly rattling around in that great barn of a place. It's nothing to me now. I have an apartment, and we'll be moving in tonight."

Dr. Larson looked him in the eye and asked again, "Where is it?"

Aloysius grinned and offered him a cigar, knowing full well that he smoked only cigarettes. However, Dr. Larson accepted it, and Aloysius so far forgot himself as to ask peevishly, "What's the matter with you? You know you don't smoke cigars."

"I hand them out to my patients," Dr. Larson said composedly. "The ones I allow to smoke cigars, that is. They appreciate little attentions of that sort. It's good for business."

Virginia stood up and announced that she'd have to get back to the office. She left without ceremony, feeling furious at both of them—at her father, because he had sold their house and lost the cook and first floor worker, no laundry, along with it, and at Dr. Larson simply because he was a Larson, and therefore a traditional enemy of the Grahams. She walked slowly through the heat and glare of Main Street, her eyes on the ground and her brows drawn together by an irritated frown. She would have gone straight past Susan Falks, except for the fact that Susan's white stockings and white, businesslike oxfords drew her eyes up.

They exchanged greetings, and Virginia thought that the brown curls and laughing blue eyes had an unusually downcast air, something approximating her own mood.

"Anything wrong?" she asked directly.

Susan made a little face. "I've been looking at a room, and I wish you could see it. Ten dollars a week, and the bed and I can hardly get in there together. I guess I'll have to take it, though. Aunt Florence says I'll have to give up my room because Aunt Alice is coming next week, and I have to live somewhere. But ten dollars a week for just that miserable little room! I'll have to eat out, and I can't really afford it. But what on earth am I to do?"

Virginia gazed for a while into the palm-filled window of H. Becker, Mortician, without really seeing it, and then turned back to Susan with sudden resolution.

"Don't take that room, Sue. Father and I have an apartment, and you can live with us as our guest."

Susan gasped and then let out an ecstatic squeal. "Oh, Virginia! Honestly? No fooling? That's simply wonderful! But where is it?"

"Hush!" Virginia said hastily. "It's a—well, it's a secret. You're

not to tell anybody, not one soul, or we won't get it. Just meet us at
ten o'clock tonight in front of the town hall with one small suitcase and
nothing more."

Susan promised eagerly, and they parted. She was immensely
relieved to have secured a place to live and pleasurably excited at
being involved in a mystery, and she walked on air all the way back to
her job, which was office nurse to Dr. Larson. She could not help
telling him, when he came in, that she had at last found a place to live,
and it took him exactly three minutes to get the whole story out of her.

So, when ten o'clock struck that night, there were not three people
standing in front of the city hall with small suitcases, but four.

When they had sorted themselves out, and the fifth wheel was
revealed as Dr. Larson, Virginia turned angrily on Susan.

"How could you tell him when you promised so faithfully not to
say a word to anyone! Now it'll be all over town, and we won't be
able to keep the place."

Susan could only giggle helplessly while Aloysius furiously informed
the interloper that they would not "move one step in any direction until
he had gone home and got into bed."

"I have no home," Dr. Larson said, shifting his suitcase and a
raincoat from one arm to the other.

"Don't quibble," Aloysius said firmly. "Just go."

There was a short silence, and then Dr. Larson turned away dejectedly.

"Four rooms and storage space," he muttered bitterly, "and you
won't even fit me in with the trunks."

The Grahams met this pathos with hearts of stone, but Susan whispered, "Oh, let him come. Surely we can find room for him."

Dr. Larson paused to see whether this appeal met with any encouragement, but when it became obvious that the other two were
unmoved, he continued on his way.

He did not go far. No farther, in fact, than the next corner, where
he leaned against the granite side of the town bank and peered around
its edge.

To his surprise, the three conspirators did not make for a car, but
started out on foot. They doubled back behind the town hall and filed
silently into the woods.

Dr. Larson had no trouble in following them, and after a few minutes he knew where they were going. He laughed quietly to himself for some time. There would be a really fancy display of fireworks when Maude and Una discovered that menagerie in their left wing.

He felt a few weak twinges of conscience when he supposed that he really should not have any part in the business, but after all, if they were discovered and he lost Maude and Una as patients, it wouldn't ruin him. And anyway, it would annoy the Grahams to have him living with them.

The terrace could be seen now, with the left wing rising dimly behind it, and he stopped in the shadow of a tree and watched Aloysius boost the two girls over the white picket fence. This seemed to be accomplished with ease, but when Aloysius attempted to vault lightly over, himself, he failed three times in a row. He snarled softly, "I did it this morning, and I can do it now," but Dr. Larson took pity on him and, stepping out from behind his tree, gave him a boost.

It was an altruistic gesture, but it failed badly. Aloysius leaped silently and convulsively into the air and landed heavily, still on the wrong side of the fence.

"It's all right," Dr. Larson said in a low voice. "I was merely trying to help."

Aloysius breathed heavily for a while, and when he spoke, it was with restrained violence.

"I might have known it would be you. Trying to scare me into a heart attack and pushing yourself in where you're not wanted."

"You may call me Jim," Dr. Larson said graciously, "and I'd like the girls to call me Jim, as well. Makes it more homelike, when we're all living together. Here, give me your foot, and I'll boost you over."

"Get out of here and go home," Aloysius hissed through his teeth. "You're trespassing."

"So are you. Come on, we'd better not waste any more time, or we'll be discovered and thrown out before we're fairly in."

Aloysius recognized and accepted defeat, and in grim silence allowed himself to be helped over the fence. It did nothing for his rapidly mounting temper to see the self-styled Jim place one hand on the top of the fence and fly gracefully over on the first try.

Virginia and Susan were quarreling in undertones about Susan's broken promise when Aloysius reached the French doors, and he savagely ordered them to shut up while he fumbled in his pocket for the key. He experienced a moment of horror when he thought he had lost it, and then his fingers closed over it and he breathed again.

They herded into the blackness of the large living room, and Aloysius gave orders for everyone to find all windows and pull the shades.

"They're dark shades—I noticed them this morning," he explained self-importantly. "When they're down, we can put on a light."

Once the shades were drawn, there was a good deal of fumbling around in the dark and an occasional hysterical giggle from Susan. Aloysius found an electric switch, but when he pressed it there was no answering flood of light. In the end, Virginia found a lamp that worked to the extent of throwing a faint glow through its dark silk shade, and Aloysius rubbed his hands together with satisfaction.

"Now! What do you think of this for a living room? Not bad, eh?"

"It's a good thing those shades are dark," Virginia commented, apparently unimpressed.

"Which room does Oliver P.'s spirit hang out in?" Jim asked, looking about him.

Susan screamed, and they all sprang at her, clapping their various hands over her mouth.

Aloysius felt a surge of anger and exasperation. It was just like Virginia to rush off and ask that stupid Susan in here, and Susan must needs drag that Larson oaf into it too. It was no use, he thought bitterly, having brilliant ideas, when people were always waiting around, ready to muck them up.

He caught Virginia by the arm and swung her toward the stairs. "You'd better come up and grab a bedroom before they're all taken. And it would serve you right if they were."

He started up the stairs himself, and felt the other three pushing close behind him. But he knew the layout and was able to walk with dignity into one of the rooms with a double bed and shut the door in all their faces.

Nevertheless, he was still angry. It would have been a beautiful arrangement for just the two of them, and now the place was all cluttered up with people he didn't like. He listened, and gathered that the girls had established themselves in the room with the twin beds, while Larson took the remaining room with the double bed, which adjoined his own and had a connecting door. He carefully lowered the window shades and then tried the overhead lights, but apparently there were no bulbs in the bracket. He remembered that there was a bedside lamp, and he made his way to it, but it would not work, either, although there was a bulb in it.

He was infuriated just then to see a line of light under the door leading to Larson's room. He wanted to slam through the door and bust Larson in the nose, but instead he went to bed in the dark and lay stewing on a bare mattress and the coarse ticking of the uncovered pillow. However, it was a good pillow and a comfortable mattress, and since it was a warm night, he needed no cover other than the silken bedspread. He wallowed drowsily and was just drifting off to sleep when the bedside light went on.

CHAPTER 4

ALOYIUS HAD a wild moment when he thought that the hand of Oliver P.'s ghost had turned on the light, and he had to tell himself not to be a fool even while the sweat started out of his forehead. It was the bulb, he thought shakily, a defective bulb that would light up if you tapped it or something shook it, or just for no particular reason at all.

He stretched out his arm and switched the light off, but he lay for a long time, telling himself about defective bulbs he had known, before he was able to get to sleep, and he slept late and heavily in the morning, while the others got up and went off to their various jobs.

They had brought no food with them, and so they had to walk into the town to get breakfast. It was cool and pleasant in the woods, and Susan giggled from sheer lightheartedness.

"This will be hard going in winter, though," she suggested. "We'll have to get snowshoes or something."

"You're looking too far ahead," Virginia said practically. "This is only June, and if we don't have a proper place to live by fall, Maude and Una will have discovered us and thrown us out, anyway."

Susan sighed. "I hope they don't discover us for a long while. I love that room."

"We ought to be paying rent," Jim said thoughtfully. "If we could pay rent and get a receipt for it, they couldn't dispossess us."

Virginia flicked him a cold glance. "Talk sense. And don't forget that you and Susan are merely guests. The apartment belongs to Father, because he found it first."

"I'm a paying guest," Jim said, and pulled out his wallet.

"You put that away," Virginia replied quickly. "I'm not running a rooming house, and you'll keep your own room clean. In fact, you'll do your share of the general housework."

"Surely we could get someone to do the work?"

Susan laughed gaily. "Oh, Jim, you are silly. How long do you think we'd keep our secret? But don't worry about it, I'll help you—"

"You will not," Virginia interposed firmly. "We all have to work during the day, and we're all going to do a fair share when we get home."

"What about Aloysius?" Jim asked. "He has nothing to do all day. Why can't he do the housework?"

Virginia compressed her lips and shook her head. "The most I've ever been able to get out of him is the marketing and a few other little odd jobs, and I don't intend to waste my time attempting the impossible."

"But that's illogical—"

"Illogical or not, that's the way it is. Now, tonight we'll have to clean the place up. It's filthy with dust, and we'll all have to pitch in. When it's clean, we can divide the work and do it at our own convenience. And don't think, Jim Larson, that you can get out of your share by not showing up tonight, because it won't work. I know how lazy men are about housework."

"You shouldn't judge other men by your father," Jim said with dignity. "I had every intention of showing up tonight, and I'm a fast and thorough worker, whether it's housework or tonsil snatching."

They had emerged onto Main Street, and Susan exclaimed suddenly, "Look! There's old Doc Hanson, up and about in the early hours of the morning. If I had his money, I'd have breakfast in bed, and not bother to get up for lunch, either."

Jim squinted into the sunshine at the tall, thin figure across the street and grinned faintly.

"He has dedicated his life to healing the halt, the lame, and the blind."

"I always heard he wouldn't do eye work," Susan said absently.

They all called good morning as they passed, and Dr. Hanson bowed with a certain amount of reserve. He was forty-nine, and he would have been astonished and mortified if he had known that they called him "old Doc Hanson." He had worked long and hard during the war, handling the town and countryside by himself, and it was a relief to have the young fellow take up some of the burden. He ought to feel completely satisfied, and yet he couldn't. Young Larson had only the experience he had gained in the Army, and it made Hanson uneasy to see some of his oldest patients going there. If only he could have handed over certain patients and kept the ones he wanted to keep. But it didn't work that way, of course. Some of the foremost people had switched, simply because they were old friends of the Larson family.

"Silly fools," Dr. Hanson thought bitterly. "Taking chances with their health for the sake of friendship."

He turned into the little paper shop to buy some cigars. Ten cents each. He could afford it, of course, but it was a fearful price—outrageous. He thought again, as he had thought frequently of late, that he ought to raise his fees. He'd do it, too, except that he knew with deadly certainty that there would be a perfect stampede over to Larson.

He put the cigars into his pocket and walked back to his long, low, shining car. Everything had gone up in price, every mortal thing, and yet he could not raise his fees, because everyone in town knew he had money, and they'd all rise up in fury. It wasn't fair when he was working for practically nothing. Probably he didn't—in fact, you could count it out—he didn't make as much per hour as a factory hand.

He started the car and it leaped away from the curb, spitting gravel viciously from its rear wheels. He drove straight to the Graham house, where Maude admitted him with an indifferent, "Hello, Bert. Come on in and have some coffee with us. We've just finished the breakfast dishes."

She preceded him through the hall and into the large kitchen. She was a tall, dark-haired woman, handsome and with odd, sleepy, yellow-green eyes. Her sister Una stood at the sink. She was dark-haired too, but smaller and slighter, and her eyes were a smoky gray.

Bert put his hat down on a table and noticed, too late, that its surface was smeared with jam. He retrieved the hat and frowned at the streaks of jam which now decorated the underside of the brim.

Una looked over and exclaimed, "Oh, I'm sorry, Bert. Here, wipe it off with this."

She handed him a dirty dishrag with which she had been wiping off the tops of the tables, but he backed away, while the frown deepened. He had no intention of touching the soiled thing, much less of wiping off his good panama with it.

Maude had gone to the stove, but she now turned around and took in the situation with a glance. She walked over, snatched the hat from Bert's hand, and washed the jam off by the simple expedient of holding it under the running faucet in the sink.

Bert gave a gasp of pure horror, but Maude wiped the hat off with a towel and handed it back to him.

"Now, don't start fussing, Bertram. You can afford a dozen panamas if you want them, and anyway the thing's as good as new."

She rattled cups and saucers onto one of the tables, and when Una had brought cookies and the coffeepot, they sat down together.

"Are you here for business or pleasure?" Una asked, breaking a cookie into pieces but making no attempt to eat it.

"How could I be here on business," Bert said, looking annoyed, "when you give it all to Jim Larson?"

"Oh, cut it out, Bert," Maude said impatiently. "You know perfectly well that we went to him to lead some of the patients there, so that you could ease up. Why don't you retire now that the war is over? Look at you—thin as a rake. You ought to quit and take a trip around the world. In fact, you could take Una and me with you. We'll show you the ropes in return for our expenses."

Bert's thin lips worked for a few moments of silence and then he managed a smile which made him look as though he were being strangled. "Great idea," he murmured, looking into the depths of his coffee cup.

Wister's bedroom door opened suddenly and he appeared, attired in a dressing gown.

"You know I can't sleep with you all talking here," he said querulously.

Maude looked up at him. "Oh, sorry. We'll move into—" She was cut off abruptly as Una slid quietly to the floor and lay still.

CHAPTER 5

BERT TOOK CHARGE in the absence of Una's own doctor and because it was an emergency, as he explained rather formally to Maude, who merely begged him to stop gibbering and get on with it.

Una was revived and put to bed, and Maude accompanied Bert downstairs again. In the front hall he paused and turned to her with a little frown.

"She's run down—needs rest and care and careful attention to the diet. You had better get her own doctor in to look her over."

"Oh, come off it, Bert," Maude said impatiently. "I've explained why we went to Larson, and you go around pouting, instead of being grateful."

Bert's face took on an injured expression. "That's all very well, but it doesn't help my reputation. It looks as though I hadn't taken care of you properly. And what makes it worse is that your family and the Larsons have always been at odds."

"That's another thing in its favor," Maude said promptly. "It's time someone broke up a silly, senseless feud like that one. In fact, we're killing two birds with one stone."

"You're going to kill more than a bird with that stone," Bert muttered angrily.

But Maude merely went off into a gale of laughter, so that he jammed the panama onto his head and sought his car in the driveway.

Maude watched him for a while and reflected that despite his extreme respect for money, if you wanted to put it that way, Bert always had been a sucker for a fancy car. She continued to watch until the present resplendent model had rolled off down the drive, and then she retired within to do some housework. But her mind was on her sister, and when she presently knocked over a silver vase, spilling water and flowers, she muttered furiously, "Damn Una, anyway. She's a miserable, weak sissy."

She glimpsed Wister in one of the other rooms, busy over some housework of his own, and called sharply, "Wister! For God's sake, go back to bed. You can't work day and night."

"With Miss Una sick, there's too much for you to do alone."

"Nonsense! I'm doing no more than is absolutely necessary. You go on back to bed. If you get sick, I'll have to look after you, and then the house certainly will go to rack and ruin."

Wister said mildly, "I got home fairly early last night, so I was able to get some sleep. I feel all right."

"You get to bed at once. It's not much after nine, and you couldn't have come in before four."

"No, Miss Maude, but I'm not doing anything much. I just want to finish this—"

Maude took the duster out of his hand and said briefly, "I'll finish it. Now, go to bed."

Wister retired with puckered brow and obvious reluctance, and as soon as he had gone, Maude threw the duster into a closet, muttering, "The old maid!"

She went out to the kitchen and began to make coffee, moving quietly so that Wister would not hear and start worrying because she had not got all the dust out of the intricate carving of the old chest in the library. She furnished a small tray and carried it up the back stairs, along the wide upper hall, to Una's luxurious bedroom.

Una, lying on her back in the wide bed, looked small and frail, and her eyes were dark with fear or trouble. She turned her head a little and saw the tray.

"Oh, Maude, you shouldn't have bothered. Look, it isn't ten o'clock yet, and this is our third coffee."

"Well, why not?" Maude demanded. "There's nothing like a good strong cup of coffee to keep you going, and I have to vacuum the blasted carpets today or Wister will wash them with his tears."

Una laughed and propped herself up with a couple of pillows.

"You know, we should get us two more husbands, with money, and then we'd be all right."

"Ah, husbands!" Maude said scornfully. "Pests! It won't be long now before we'll have plenty of money. All we have to do is hang on and stick it out."

Una put her cup carefully back onto its saucer and shivered. Maude frowned at her.

"Don't be such a milksop. I can't for the life of me see why it gets you down so. Everything is all right. Bert's dying to prescribe a tonic for you. Maybe I'll ask him for one, secretly. It'll put him in a better humor anyway and it might even do you some good."

"Perhaps one of us had better marry him," Una said, fingering the delicate old silver teaspoon in her Crown Derby saucer.

Maude hooted with laughter. "Imagine being married to that old stick!" she screamed.

Una continued to play with the spoon and observed, without raising her eyes, "The old stick has money."

"Oh, to hell with money," Maude said carelessly. "What do you want now? I'll sell something and buy it for you."

"I want a better life than this."

"You *had* a better life and that didn't suit you, either. When you say one of us had better marry Bert that means you, because I wouldn't have him wrapped in tissue paper and satin ribbon, and you know it. And how the devil you could leave a man like Randall and then contemplate Bert is beyond me."

"Oh, Ed was horrid!" Una cried petulantly. "You know he was."

Maude leaned back in her chair and sipped her coffee in silence. Una was spoiled, she thought. Everyone had spoiled her, even Ed Randall, and probably that was why she had left him. And here she sat herself, continuing to spoil her. She was only five years older than Una, but she felt immeasurably more mature.

She thought of her own husband, rushing off to the war like a young kid as soon as they would take him, and he'd been forty-five at the time. Old enough to know better. He'd been killed almost right away and had left nothing except her war-widow pension. That came in handy, of course. She wished she'd been able to keep him at home but he wouldn't listen to her. They'd both been forty-five, and she hadn't realized that they were not still a young couple. She was fifty now, though, and felt every year of it.

Una put the tray off her lap with a little clatter. "Please stop daydreaming and tell me why being married to Bert, with all his money, would be so bad."

Maude glanced at her and thought tolerantly, in other words, stop thinking about you, and let's talk about me. Una all over. However, she said cheerfully enough, "All right, honey, you go ahead and marry Bert if you want to. After all, if you don't like it, you can always leave him."

Una nodded. "And get alimony," she said dreamily.

Maude stood up and carried her empty cup over to the tray. "You dratted little pig! After all I've done to try and bring you up properly. You might as well cut Bert's heart out as to take alimony from him."

"Well, he always wanted to marry one of us. After all, he asked us both at different times and he's never married anyone else, so it ought to be worth it to him."

"Never mind about that," Maude said, her face suddenly serious. "I want to know why you fainted. There must have been something.. What's wrong with you lately?"

Una looked away, while one small white hand plucked nervously at the sheet.

"Come on," Maude said impatiently. "Something's eating you. I've noticed it and I want to know what it is."

She picked up the tray and waited for a moment, but there was no reply and she presently turned away.

"All right, there's no way of digging it out of you, I suppose. If you won't tell me, you won't."

She had gone as far as the door before Una spoke.

"I'm almost certain that I saw Father the other day."

CHAPTER 6

MAUDE ALMOST DROPPED the tray but was able to save it with a bit of expert juggling. She came back to the bed and asked in a queer, breathless voice, "Where?"

"Walking along Main Street."

Maude released air that had been held overlong in her lungs and said sharply, "Nonsense! How could he walk along Main Street? He's supposed to be dead."

Una's face had a pinched look, and she spoke in a low voice. "But he's different. He's grown a black goatee. I didn't notice him much at first. He was walking ahead of me and he'd stop and look at the shop windows. And then I saw his face, and it—it hit me. Maude, I could swear it was Father." Her head dropped against the pillows, and she watched her sister with scared gray eyes.

Maude gave a little shiver and muttered, "The silly old fool." She was silent for a moment and then she straightened her shoulders. "It would be just like him to think he could get away with it, after getting all that insurance." Her eyes glowed green with sudden anger. "We'd be involved, too, since we're collecting the money."

"I know," Una whispered. "Here we are, living like this, pretending to keep things up as if we had the money, and Wister working his head off at a roadhouse all night and then coming back to do more work around here."

"Wister's a fool," Maude declared. "I've told him time and again to go, but he won't. He seems to get some enjoyment out of this loyalty-to-the-old-homestead stuff, but I still say he's a fool. He has his own life to live, and he isn't so old, and not bad-looking. Well." She shrugged. "Perhaps he hits it up at night occasionally."

Una blinked over gathering tears and murmured, "I feel so defeated."

"Let's sell the house," Maude suggested, "and get out. Father will never come forward. He thinks too much of his own skin."

"Oh no!" Una cried in a terrified voice. "You know Father—you know what he's like. He'd come forward at once, in an utter fury. He might be sorry later, when we were all sitting around in jail, but that wouldn't help much. And I couldn't stand going to jail, Maude, I couldn't. Let's just stick it out and hope to God that no one else recognizes him. I might have been mistaken, you know. Perhaps it wasn't Father after all."

Maude had put the tray onto a table and, after frowning into space for a while, lighted a cigarette and began to pace the room.

"All right, Una, but you'll have to pull yourself together. You look fit to go under and it isn't worth it. Get a grip on yourself. After all, we have enough money to get by. Father can't last forever."

"Oh yes, he can," Una sobbed. "He'll last forever, and we'll be stuck here." She dabbed at her eyes with a wisp of perfumed and embroidered handkerchief. "I tell you, I can't stand it. I'm going to marry Bert."

"You're a weak sissy," Maude said flatly. "But do what you want, of course."

She picked up the tray again and carried it down to the kitchen. She washed the cups and saucers and put them away, and then went out to the garden and began to weed one of the numerous flower beds.

She had been working for some time when she glanced up and noted, without enthusiasm, that Aloysius was approaching. She bent to her weeding again and said indifferently, "Hello, Wishus."

" 'Lo, Maude," he called cheerfully. "How are you on this beautiful morning?"

"I'm all right," Maude said, looking him in the eye, "but if you've come to beg, borrow, or steal any part of our living quarters here, the answer is still no."

She tugged viciously at a weed and wished that it were her father's nose she was pulling.

There were so many empty rooms, all completely furnished, and they could be making a nice income by renting them, but the word had come through from Father: no roomers. And every time she had made up her mind to defy the old devil, Una went into hysterics. It was maddening.

"My dear Maude, don't distress yourself on my account any longer," Aloysius said with a wave of his arm. "That is," he added spitefully, "if you ever did. Virginia and I have acquired an excellent apartment and are already moved in."

"Hmm, said Maude. "That's nice. Where is it?"

Aloysius gestured vaguely. "Over there, at the other end of town."

"Where? What's the address?"

"Are those zinnias?" Aloysius asked. "Bloom in July, don't they? I believe they make very nice cut flowers for the house." Maude nodded and had told him several things about zinnias before she realized that he had changed the subject.

"Listen, Wishus. Is there any secret about this apartment you've snaffled? Where is it?"

Aloysius cleared his throat and then fell back upon attack as the best method of defense.

"Why should you be interested in where we're living?" he asked indignantly. "You didn't care what became of us. With all the empty rooms you have here, we could have been sleeping on a couple of park benches."

"You had a home," Maude said tartly, "and you sold it for profit— a huge profit, as I happen to know. Why should you expect other people to take you into their homes so that you can keep your money in your pocket and rattle it when you want to impress anybody?"

Aloysius turned and walked away. He told himself that he did not want to lose his temper, but knew all the time that he had lost it and was retreating for fear he would talk too much, the usual situation when he was in a fury. If he started sounding off to Maude, he might say something that would betray his secret and he valued his new quarters too highly to take any chances.

He walked out to Main Street and did some marketing, which put him in a good humor again. He'd cook dinner tonight, a really fine dinner. Annoyance seized him again as he remembered Susan and Jim. Should he make enough stew for both of them, or enough only for Susan, or leave them both out entirely? Well, he'd put it up to Virginia and let her decide.

He was meeting her for lunch, and when he had finished his marketing he went along to the Kuntree Koffee Shoppe, where he discovered that he was a little early. He took advantage of the fact to select a small table for two, so that no one would be tempted to sit down with them.

However, this maneuver went wrong from the outset. Before Virginia arrived, Dr. Bertram Hanson wandered in, caught sight of Aloysius, and decided that he'd better show a bit of cordiality. He'd lost one part of the Graham family and it would be bad all around if he lost the other as well.

He carefully lowered himself into Virginia's waiting chair and said genially, "Hello, Aloysius. Having a bite to eat?"

"Certainly," said Aloysius bitterly, "I've been chewing on the nap-kin."

"Eh?"

"I'm meeting Virginia. We're lunching together."

But Bert didn't get it. He picked up a menu and asked vaguely, "What's good today?"

"Nothing!" said Aloysius irritably. "We come here to keep from starving, because there's no better place in town. I'm expecting Virginia at any minute. We have a private matter to discuss."

But Bert was carefully reading down the price list. He came to an item at thirty-five cents, glanced at the left-hand column and saw that it was a cream-cheese-and-jelly sandwich, and after a moment's hesitation ordered it from the hovering waitress. Aloysius sulkily told the girl that he'd wait, and she flitted off.

Virginia came in a moment later, and Bert sprang to his feet and pulled another chair over to the table for her. She sat down, shaking back her fine, silvery-blonde hair, and then asked her father, peevishly, why he had picked out such a small table, since she hated being crowded.

Aloysius glared at Bert and said, "I had supposed there would be only the two of us."

Bert had his sandwich open, looking for the jelly, and seemed not to have heard either of them.

Virginia said, "Hush!" and ordered some creamed chicken, and the waitress flitted off again without a glance at Aloysius. But Aloysius had always made it a rule to be more bully than bullied. He opened his mouth, roared loudly, and within two minutes his order had been taken with apologies and deference.

Virginia squirmed, as she always did when her father made a scene, and Bert colored and kept his eyes on his plate. He wished fervently that he had never sat down with them. It was very crowded, too—such a small table. There had been several tables from which he might have chosen when he came in.

He looked around rather absently, and suddenly his gaze sharpened and focused on a man sitting some distance away, an elderly man with black hair and a black goatee.

The color drained out of Bert's face, and his coffee spoon fell from his hand and clattered onto the table.

CHAPTER 7

VIRGINIA AND Aloysius each gave Bert a glance of reproof, but since their order appeared at that moment, they made no comment and devoted themselves to the food.

Bert felt awkward and a bit silly. He had just turned his head for another furtive look at the man in the goatee when there was a rude interruption. Dr. James Larson had come in, and after cheerfully greeting all of them and getting practically no response, he pulled up a chair and edged himself into the already overcrowded table.

Even while Bert was giving him a thin smile, he realized that he hated him. He hated his newfangled methods and the way he had breezily fooled a certain number of people into believing in them, too. But it was necessary to be civil, of course. Policy and ethics demanded it.

Bert made an effort and forced himself to ask, as though he really cared, "Have you found a place to live yet, Jimmy?"

Jim nodded. "Yes, I have. Nice place, too, but probably only temporary. I had the devil of a time getting in there, and the people would like nothing better right now than to push me out again. It was difficult for me to get in, but they'll find that it's even more difficult to get me out."

Bert was uninterested, but he asked courteously, "Where is the place?"

Jim waved an arm and said obscurely, "Around."

Bert took another look at the man with the goatee. There was no doubt about it. He was the living image of Oliver P. Graham.

Jim's order arrived, and there ensued a period of confusion. Aloysius's salad crashed to the floor and Bert's plate was summarily removed, although there was still a small piece of his sandwich left on it. Order of a sort was at length restored, although the waitress observed coldly that she was sorry but the table was intended for only two.

Aloysius said that if that were the case, they had no business permitting more than two to sit at it, and would she kindly bring him another salad at once.

Virginia said, "Shh," and Jim gave it as his opinion that a few inconveniences were well worth a gathering of congenial people.

Aloysius, glooming over the fact that the replaced salad and his apple pie would probably arrive together and spoil the proper sequence of his lunch, turned on Jim and snarled, "Save your pretty speeches for your patients. They need a few kind words while they're being helped into eternity. You sat down here to annoy us and we know it and you know it."

"Nothing of the sort. I sat down here because your lovely daughter attracts me."

Virginia said, "Shut up!" and appeared to be speaking to both of them.

Bert, who had not been listening, suddenly decided to air a grievance.

"Jimmy, I hear that you've promised to cure Mary Trummidge of her neuritis."

"I made no promise of any sort," Jim stated, immediately hot under the collar. " I merely advised her to try—"

"That's no good," Bert said sharply.

"There have been some very good results from it, excellent, and there's no reason whatever why she shouldn't try it."

"Now you listen to me," said Bert. He had much to say and said it, but Aloysius looked over at Virginia and raised an eyebrow. She nodded and they both rose from the table.

"But what about the check?" Virginia whispered as they neared the door.

"One of those neuritis experts can pay it," Aloysius said, grinning. "Teach them not to push in where they are not wanted. Now, listen, I've been marketing and I have all the supplies we need. I'm going to cook a nice little dinner tonight. But I forgot the electric-light bulbs. I had no light at all for my room last night, except one that seems to go on and off according to its own mood. So remember to bring some, will you?"

Virginia promised to see to the bulbs and Aloysius went off to the garage where he kept his car. The back seat was loaded with packages and he took them all out, balancing them precariously in his arms and feeling decidedly aggrieved that he could not save trouble by driving the car up to his door.

In the woods, about halfway between Main Street and the Graham house, he stumbled over a stone and fell flat, the packages flying in all directions. For a while he simply lay there and swore until he was faint, but when an insect of some sort began to cruise up his leg, inside his trousers, he scrambled to his feet. He found that he could not balance all the groceries in his arms again, and in the end he had to make two trips. He had just returned from the second trip, sweating and puffing, when he heard the voices of Maude and Una, somewhere in the wing.

Aloysius backed up to the wall beside the fireplace and froze, his sweaty hands still clutching the last of the packages and his heart hammering uncomfortably.

He had understood that they never came into this part of the house. He wondered wildly what they could be doing.

They were out on the stairs, and he presently gathered that they were struggling to carry something down. Maude was cursing and Una whining. Aloysius barely breathed as he heard them reach the bottom and move slowly along the hall, apparently still carrying their burden, whatever it was. There was a pause, and then the sound of a key, and they passed out of the wing, locking the door behind them.

Aloysius dropped his packages and raced up the stairs. The second floor seemed to be all right. The three bedroom doors were closed, and only a section of violet tub and lavender-tiled floor was visible in the bathroom. Alien toothbrushes and towels were hidden behind the half-closed door. He gave a grunt of satisfaction and went on up to the attic.

The portrait of Oliver P. was gone, and Aloysius nodded to himself. Probably they had sold it. It was a good painting and had cost a fancy price, although why anyone would want to waste expensive oils on a copy of the nondescript mattress face of Oliver P. was well beyond Aloysius's comprehension. The girls, he decided, showed good solid sense in selling the thing. Evidently they had had a copy made and hung it over the mantel downstairs so that Oliver's spirit would not be affronted.

Aloysius, relieved that his new quarters had not fallen in ashes about his head, laughed heartily and made his way downstairs again.

He put the groceries away behind the bar and immediately switched on both burners of the electric grill. He intended to cook an entire dinner and there was not too much time, since he could put only two saucepans on at once. He removed his coat, rolled up his sleeves, and went to work, whistling softly to himself.

In the main part of the house, in a small music room, Bert was receiving the shock of his life. Una, seated on a piano bench and frowning at her shoes, was telling him that if he still wanted to marry her, and she nearly added, "or Maude," she would now be happy to oblige.

Bert was beside himself with joy. Ever since his boyhood he had wanted to marry one of the Graham girls, but for many years they had been right out of his class. His parents had been farm people with chronic money trouble. The Grahams could be dreamed about but hardly approached. They belonged to another orbit, glamorous with social and financial prestige.

But he had made his way in the world, had money and a certain position, and if he could have a Graham for a wife, it would be the final, crowning success. He had come to the house in response to a call from Una, who had asked him to bring her a tonic.

He had been sitting on a small gilt chair, but he left it to join Una on the piano bench. He kissed her twice and vowed that he would make every effort to protect her happiness.

Maude had watched the entire proceeding from the hall. When she thought that Bert had run out of noble sentiments, she went in and offered a few languid felicitations. Bert thanked her and then announced that he intended to give Una his most prized possession, his deceased mother's engagement ring. Una's face fell, and Maude promptly came to her rescue.

"That's a very nice thought, Bert. Una will treasure it. And by the way, when you buy Una her own engagement ring, I'd better go with you, because I know what she likes."

Bert's face fell also. In the short silence that followed, the front doorbell rang. Wister appeared so promptly that Maude knew he had been listening, and was irritated. She moved out into the hall, and as

Wister opened the door, her eyes widened to their fullest extent.

Una's ex-husband, Edward Randall, stood in the doorway.

CHAPTER 8

AS FAR AS MAUDE was concerned, the sudden appearance of Ed Randall gave color and interest to an otherwise drab proceeding. She yelled a cheerful greeting and went forward to usher him inside. Una and Bert had come into the hall, and Una's face was burning with a dark flush. Bert felt himself to be in the most embarrassing position of his entire life.

Ed boomed, "Well, well, well, all the old familiar faces, eh? I'm stuck for a place to park the aging body, so I remembered you girls lived in the next town and drove over. Harya, Bert, old kid? And Una looking like a princess, as usual. Maudie, I know you'll give an old pal a bed and breakfast."

"Of course. Where's your luggage?"

"But he can't," Bert broke in feverishly. "This is outrageous."

Maude and Ed did not even hear him. Ed was exhibiting a lone suitcase and saying, "There it is—gent's complete outfit in the small economy-size package. Wister can haul it right up."

"No, he can't," Maude said. "He's our only servitor at the moment and I dare not ask him to do anything. Pick it up yourself, boy, and I'll take you upstairs and show you where to hang your hat."

"Good old Maudie," said Ed, and picked up the suitcase. They went up the stairs, Ed talking incessantly, as usual, and Maude could hear Bert bleating agitatedly below. As she led Ed to one of the dusty guest rooms, she reflected that she had not enjoyed herself so much for a long time. She got sheets from the linen closet in the hall and exhibited them with pride.

"You're lucky, brother, we don't always have sheets for our guests these days. Help me to drape the sacred things on your bed, will you?"

Ed helped with more energy than skill and told her to make up a list of whatever linens she needed, as he knew people in the right places and could get anything she wanted at wholesale prices.

"You're a blasted wonder, Ed," Maude said admiringly. "You always could get anything, and get it wholesale, too. Una was an utter dope to break up with you while we still have all these postwar shortages."

Ed glanced at the door and lowered his voice. "You know, I have an idea that Una and I could make a go of it if we were to give it another try. I think I'll make a play for her while I'm here."

"Good idea," Maude said approvingly. "Of course, she just got herself engaged to old Bert down there, but that shouldn't worry you too much."

"Luvva Pete!" Ed exclaimed in honest amazement. "I didn't think there was a red-blooded dame living who would marry that skinny old bumbershoot."

"He has a pile of money," Maude pointed out.

"Oh, sure, that would weigh with a lot of dames, but it can't mean much to Una. You girls have plenty. She wouldn't even let me pay her any alimony. Said not to bother, because it would be only a spit in the bucket."

Maude forced a smile onto her face. While she realized that although alimony from Ed might once have been a spit in the bucket, it sounded now more like a nice little ocean. She shrugged and said hastily, "Oh no—Una isn't marrying Bert for his money."

Ed jerked one end of the top sheet out from under his foot and sent it sailing across the bed.

"Maudie, you can't tell me that Una is marrying that monkey for love."

"You'd better ask *her*, Ed. I don't know."

They got the bed made between them. Maude picked up the bureau scarf and dusted the room a bit with it.

"Never can find a duster," she said absently. "I believe Wister keeps them all nice and clean and then hides them somewhere so we won't dirty them."

They presently went downstairs together, companionably arm in arm, and found Una and Bert waiting for them at the bottom.

Bert stepped forward and cleared his throat. "I think you should know, Randall, that Una and I are engaged to be married and I feel that it would be unconventional, to say the least, if you were to stay here overnight."

Maude couldn't help laughing, and Ed said amiably, "It would look worse than unconventional if I slept out on the lawn, brother. I gave up wearing pajamas ten years ago."

Bert cleared his throat again. "I realize, of course, the difficulty of getting accommodations just now, so I have arranged to put you up for the night at my own home."

"For heaven's sake stop fussing," Maude interposed. "Do you want to make yourself look ridiculous, Bert? Una and Ed are divorced, so that it's just as though an old friend had come to visit us, and, personally, I'm glad to have him. He's going to stay, so you might as well relax."

Ed looked vastly relieved, Una tried to look troubled but didn't seem to have her mind on it much, and Bert was scarlet in the face. He knew he was defeated, because he knew Maude only too well.

In the end, he turned and ran, with only a muttered excuse about having to see a patient. Actually he went straight home. He crossed his immaculate front lawn and was infuriated to find some crab grass growing there. He summoned Mr. Anderson, his gardener-chauffeur-butler, and rebuked him, but Mr. Anderson wasn't taking any rebukes and said so, and Bert had to go on to the house with his feelings still seething unrelieved inside him.

The house was a thorn in his side, too. He had added wings to it in an effort to make it look like a mansion. The result, however, was not a mansion, but merely a house with two foreign bodies clinging to its sides.

He thought of Una and felt better at once. Una's home was a real mansion and he'd be master there. Now that Oliver P. was dead, the place needed a master. Queer how that old man in the Koffee Shoppe had looked like Oliver, even with the clump of black hair on his chin. Oliver had always been clean-shaven though his hair had been black right up to the time of his death. It certainly was an uncanny resemblance.

Bert took off his coat and vest and lay down in the living room for a nap. He closed his eyes determinedly and tried to make his mind a blank, and then the doorbell rang. Bert opened his eyes and listened, but there was no sound of Mrs. Anderson, his housekeeper, leaving her kitchen. The bell rang again, and he realized, with impotent fury, that she knew he had come home and figured he could answer the door himself.

He got off the couch and began to button himself into his vest. He could not understand why he had such trouble with servants. He treated them well and certainly he paid them well. He paid them too much, as a matter of fact, far too much. As soon as conditions had changed enough to make it possible, he intended to lower their salaries.

He went to the front door, flung it open, and found himself face to face with Aloysius Graham.

"Hello, Bert," Aloysius said cheerfully. "Could you let me have some salt?"

"Salt!" Bert repeated, astounded.

Aloysius walked in. "Well, er, yes. Matter of fact, Bert, I'm in a bit of a hurry. I've been visiting over this way. I promised to get salt but I forgot all about it. I know you won't mind. I'll return it tomorrow."

He walked through to the kitchen, and Bert followed, feeling irritated and uneasy. He did not like people who borrowed food.

Mrs. Anderson received Aloysius with the utmost cordiality. She brought him an unopened container of the finest table salt and then insisted that he take a rhubarb pie which had just come out of the oven. She had had too much rhubarb, she explained carelessly, and so had to make too many pies.

Aloysius was delighted and appeared not to notice the horror on Bert's face. Bert was thinking, rather wildly, that the salt could be returned, but a freshly baked rhubarb pie was pure loss. He fretted between reproving Mrs. Anderson before Aloysius or waiting until he had gone.

While he hesitated, Aloysius said a courtly good-by and made for the front door, and Bert felt duty bound to accompany him. By the time he got there he realized that he dared not rebuke Mrs. Anderson, and he felt that his great happiness in being engaged to Una was being marred by countless small irritations.

Aloysius hurried off, pleased with his loot but anxious about the stew he had left simmering on the electric burner.

He hastened through the woods and climbed the picket fence with very little trouble and no damage to the pie. He went into the cool space of the living room and suddenly stopped in his tracks with his heart turning over.

An elderly man, with black hair and a black goatee, was sitting in one of the armchairs. He glanced up at Aloysius and said quietly, "I was told that I could find lodgings here."

CHAPTER 9

ALOYSIUS, already flushed and perspiring, turned a darker red and, in the heat of his emotions, was able only to sputter.

The black-haired man looked at him in mild surprise and explained, "I was at the hotel, but they would not permit me to remain there for longer than five days and my business here is not yet finished."

Aloysius became articulate and thundered, "Who sent you here? Who was it?"

"Why, Dr. Larson's office nurse. I went to him for a little chronic trouble I have, and I was telling her of my unfortunate situation. She was very kind and told me of this place. It seems very nice, but I don't like the necessity of climbing that picket fence. You should put a gate in there. I'm not as young as I was, and I don't believe it's doing you any good, either. You look a trifle apoplectic."

"I can see that the place won't suit you," Aloysius said furiously. "I'm not putting a gate in the fence, see? We all climb over, but I can see that you're used to a red carpet and an awning, so you'd better go elsewhere."

The man stood up, advanced on, Aloysius, and patted him kindly on the shoulder.

"My dear sir, no offense, no offense at all. A large stone on each side of the fence will make the climb considerably easier. I shall attend to it myself."

Aloysius stalked over to the bar and relieved himself of the pie and the salt. He silently cursed Susan and then Virginia for having told Susan in the first place. Between them they had ruined a perfect setup. He peered into the simmering stew and then said resignedly, "Come on and help me with the dinner."

The stranger joined him at once and went to work with a will that entirely placated Aloysius. He said that his name was P.X. Smith and that he was a lawyer. He was looking into a private matter in the town and was uncertain as to when he would be able to finish up the affair. In turn Aloysius explained about the Graham girls and how he had appropriated the unused wing in sheer desperation. By the time Virginia and Susan came home, the two were like old friends.

Virginia had scolded Susan all the way home for letting P.X. into their secret, and Susan had defended herself by saying that if Virginia had seen the piteous expression on the old man's face, she would have done the same. Virginia denied it scornfully, until she met P.X. Smith, and then was surprised to find herself almost immediately in a more tolerant mood. He was such a courtly old gentleman.

Aloysius gave Susan a furious glare, but she stepped behind Virginia.

The two girls went off to freshen themselves before dinner, and Aloysius called a warning after them to be quiet. They crept up the stairs and went into their room, where they flung themselves onto the two beds and lit cigarettes.

"I have a date," Susan said, blowing smoke at the ceiling. "Tomorrow night. With Gus."

Virginia inhaled deeply and said, "Mmm."

"I'm so thrilled."

"Where are you meeting him?" Virginia asked with sudden suspicion.

"Now, don't start worrying all over again. I said I'd be working late and for him to pick me up at the office."

Virginia said, "Hmm."

"You're not actually bubbling over with interest," Susan complained. "You know I always like to hear about your love affairs."

"I haven't any."

"Well, that's because you always go sounding off about how children should be brought up in nursery schools, and the wife ought to keep on with her job, and all that sort of stuff."

"My beauty and personality should shine triumphant through all that."

"Well, sure. But all that talk you give out with is apt to scare the men."

"Sissies."

Susan burrowed her head into the pillow and sighed. "Gus keeps hinting about marriage."

"Why doesn't he come right out with it?"

"Oh, give him time."

"Give you time, you mean," Virginia said.

Susan pouted up at the ceiling. "It's like I've just been telling you. You're too outspoken. You should pay some attention to the little refinements of life."

Virginia crushed out her cigarette and swung her feet off the bed. "I pay attention to three refinements a day—breakfast, lunch, and dinner. Let's go down and attend to refinement number three."

Susan giggled. "Is your father really trying to cook a meal? I mean, won't we have to go out afterwards and get something to eat?"

"Of course not. Father cooks very well when he wants to. Just because he's a man it doesn't mean that he can't do that sort of slavey work. It's only prejudice of long standing that maintains that only a woman can handle the womanly arts. And what are the womanly arts? All the dirty work—"

"All right, all right," Susan said hastily. "Come on and get your dinner, and shut up."

They descended into the heat of a sharp discussion between Aloysius and P.X. Smith. Jim had come in and was watching in silent enjoyment.

"My family has been making coffee as it should be made for sixty years, sir," P.X. was saying, his black goatee quivering with rage, "and you have the effrontery to tell me not to put in any salt!"

Jim cleared his throat and said pacifically, "Never mind, Mr. Smith. You do it your way, and I'm sure we'll all enjoy it."

Aloysius turned on Jim and furiously demanded that he mind his own business, and why wasn't he off on it, anyway? What was he hanging around for?

"I'm waiting for dinner," Jim explained simply.

"That's what I thought you were doing," Aloysius snarled. "Do you think I'm running a blasted boardinghouse?"

"You have enough stew for everybody," Jim pointed out, "and Mr. Smith seems to be staying."

"I invited Mr. Smith to stay, but I didn't invite you. I'd rather see my stew dead in the garbage can than being shoveled into your ugly puss!"

"Shut up, Father," Virginia said firmly. "There's enough food for everyone, and we owe Dr. Larson a meal. He must have paid for our lunch."

"As a matter of fact, I did," Jim admitted. "When Bert and I discovered that we had been left holding the bag, he screamed in horror and threw the check at me. He assured me over and over again, after he had calmed down, that you were honest people and would certainly pay me back."

"Well, we're not gonna," Aloysius said happily. "When people intrude on us, they can damn well pay for the pleasure of our company." He glanced around and shouted suddenly, "Hey! What's the matter with all you zombies? Why isn't there a table set? Here's the dinner all ready. I've been working on it for hours, and nobody even bothers to set the table."

It turned out to be a little difficult. There was no table large enough for them all. When they had at last found two tables that could be pushed together, there was no tablecloth. Aloysius was all for putting the meal straight onto the smooth, mellow glow of the mahogany surface, but Virginia refused to permit it, for fear of damage, and eventually Jim produced a newspaper.

But there was no cutlery of any sort. Aloysius, looking feverishly behind the bar, found some glass stems for stirring tall drinks, and declared, in the face of a solid wall of opposition, that if the Chinese could eat with chopsticks, other people could learn to do it too.

There ensued a certain amount of bickering, and at last Jim volunteered to go around to the kitchen, engage Wister in conversation, and see what he could pick up. They let him go at last, although Aloysius was sure that he'd make some silly mistake and expose them all.

Jim went quietly around to the back of the house and found the kitchen door open and the screen door unlatched. He went in, still without making any noise, and found the kitchen orderly and deserted. The door to Wister's bedroom was half closed, but a movement of some sort inside the room drew his eyes to it. He went a little closer and could see Wister standing in front of an open drawer in a bureau.

He was counting money, and Jim saw, with surprise, that they were hundred dollar bills and there seemed to be at least eight or nine of them.

CHAPTER 10

JIM BACKED AWAY from Wister's door quietly and began to open drawers at random. He tried three without finding what he wanted, but the fourth contained stacks of kitchen cutlery, and he lifted out a handful and fled.

Back in the left wing, he found them all seated around the table, and all, with one exception, staring gloomily at the appetizing stew on their plates. Aloysius was endeavoring to convey stew from his plate to his mouth with two of the glass stems, and meeting with no success. He was swearing quietly but steadily.

Jim was hailed with enthusiasm and everyone cheered up as they started to eat. Aloysius, abandoning the glass stems reluctantly, because he hated to be defeated, declared that it was exactly like old Oliver P. to have dishes and cups but no cutlery. "Probably slopped the food into his mouth with his fingers, the old bastard."

"Father!" Virginia said peremptorily. "I won't have you talking that way in front of Susan."

Susan giggled, and Jim asked, "What about me? I'm not so much older than Susan."

"You," Virginia said, "can damn well take care of your blasted self."

"You're a bit too like your old man," Jim said mildly. "Fortunately, you don't look like him, but this swearing is not seemly in a young and attractive girl. From Aloysius it seems only natural, because he is of coarser grain."

"You attend to your own culture," Aloysius said, shortly, "and I'll thank you to allow me to bring up my own daughter as I see fit."

"She's already brought up," Jim replied, "and a bad job of work it was, too."

"Now, don't explode, Father," Virginia interposed. "He's only an unwanted and uninvited guest, and he's talking through his hat because he's jealous."

"He may be talking through his hat," Aloysius said sourly, "but he's eating through his mouth. He's had more than anyone."

Jim sat back with a satisfied sigh and lit a cigarette. "Who invited me to this meal, anyway?"

"Nobody, by hell," Aloysius said, glooming at the empty stew dish.

"I believe you're right. I'm sorry, it must have been an oversight on my part."

Susan giggled, and P.X. Smith, after a puzzled glance at their faces to see whether they were serious, changed the subject by suggesting a game of poker.

Susan did not play, but the others were ready and willing, and Susan told them to go ahead, because she had some washing to do, anyhow. She added, in case there should be any mistake about it, that she did not mean the dishes.

After a certain amount of bickering, they all washed the dishes together, and Jim was sent back with the borrowed cutlery. He was unable to deliver it, as it happened, because Maude and Una were in the kitchen washing their own dishes while Ed Randall dried them.

Jim returned to the left wing, explained the situation, and promised to take the cutlery back at some other time,. They sat down to their game of poker. Susan went upstairs with some sheets and pillowcases which she and Virginia had brought and wondered idly whether she ought to remind Virginia that they had planned to clean the wing up this evening. Only Virginia seemed to be enjoying her game, and after all, they could clean the place some other time.

She made her bed and Virginia's, and then dusted a little with a towel from the bathroom. She could not find any brooms or mops and decided that they'd have to buy some. She went into Aloysius's room and found the bedspread tumbled untidily on the mattress. She clicked her tongue and shook her head a little. The rest of them had to work, and he had the day to himself, and you'd think he'd at least spread his bed up neatly.

It was growing dark, and she turned the switch of the bedside lamp, but although there was a bulb, it did not light. She twisted the bulb and slapped at it, but there was no response, so she shrugged and turned away.

She did a little dusting and then made up the bed with the fresh sheets. It was a huge bed, with carved mahogany posts—probably an antique, Susan thought, and wrinkled her nose. She didn't care for antiques. The room was large, too, and handsomely furnished. She supposed it had been Oliver P.'s room, and she wondered whether he'd died here in this great mahogany bed, and then she shivered and tried to think of something else.

She turned her mind determinedly to how she would furnish her own home when she had one. All new stuff, and pretty, but no carving or frills. Everything had to be useful.

She finished dusting and stood there for a moment and could not help thinking of Oliver P. again. No one had used this room since his death, and she wondered, in a confused way, whether he minded Aloysius being here.

As though in answer to the question in her mind, the light went on.

Susan gasped. There was no one else in the room, nobody at all, and the lamp was some distance away from her. She gave a muffled little cry and fled.

She went back to her own room and started to prepare for bed, but she was distinctly nervous. She told herself several times that there was no accounting for the vagaries of light switches, and still she could not get it out of her head that Oliver P.'s ghostly hand had turned on that lamp.

She got into a robe and slippers at last and, with a book tucked under her arm, went downstairs. As she passed Aloysius's room she saw, with a little shiver, that the light was off again.

Downstairs in the living room she tried to tell the poker players about the lamp, but the game had developed into a grim, serious battle, and not one of them so much as turned a head. Jim was losing, and the others were fighting bitterly to win the major portion of what he once, with pathos, termed his hard-earned money. He was more relaxed than any of them, since he had reached the point beyond despair.

Susan, glancing about the room, suddenly discovered that they had not pulled the dark shades. "Oh, you damn fools!" she exclaimed, yanking them down. "What next?"

No one paid her the slightest attention, and she felt almost lonely. She lay down on a couch with two pillows behind her head, began to read, and was sound asleep within five minutes.

Virginia had set a time limit for the poker game and insisted upon stopping when the time came, although Aloysius wanted to go on. They pushed back from the table, and P.X. Smith darted to a corner, picked up his bag, and was right in amongst them as they mounted the stairs. He asked them if someone would be kind enough to show him to his room.

Aloysius took charge at once, since he was well aware that if he made one false move, he'd have P.X. sleeping beside him in Oliver R.'s huge bed.

"There are no rooms left," he declared firmly, "but you can sleep on the couch in the living room. I believe that girl is there at the moment, but we'll wake her and send her off to bed."

P.X. was indignant. "But you should have told me! You never mentioned that there were no rooms. You should have told me when I first came."

"I never like to turn people away in these trying times," Aloysius said largely. "You should be thankful for a soft couch instead of a park bench. We're not running a hotel or a rooming house, you know. But my daughter and I come from generations of truly hospitable forebears, and naturally we will accept no money from you."

P.X., properly crushed, apologized and gave profuse thanks for the couch.

They returned to the living room, roused Susan, and formally handed the couch over to P.X. Aloysius gave him a few instructions about not wandering outside in the morning or opening or leaning out of windows, and then they went upstairs again.

Left to himself, P.X. watched them out of sight, wondering, without too much interest, whether Aloysius was or was not a trifle cracked. When they had gone, he undressed and lay down on the couch in his pajamas. It was fortunate, he thought, that the weather was so warm, for he had no cover of any sort. Still, he was comfortable enough.

Peculiar setup, this. Susan had told him that they were all living here without the knowledge of anyone in the main part of the house, but he found it a little hard to believe.

He dozed and was brought sharply awake again by a sound out in the hall. He raised his head, staring through the darkness, and suddenly the light went on out there. He blinked, trying to focus his eyes, and saw a dark figure cross the hall, swiftly and silently, and start up the stairs.

P.X. got quietly off the couch and followed.

CHAPTER 11

ALOYSIUS LAY ON his back in bed, but he could not sleep. He was thoroughly annoyed with Virginia because she had forgotten the electric-light bulbs and he wanted to read. He had an interesting book, and he was not sleepy.

It was all right for the rest of them, he thought angrily. They had lights in their rooms which they could turn on and off at will, so why should they bother remembering to get bulbs? And all the sympathy he had got out of them was their several observations that it was just his hard luck. He'd had first choice of bedrooms, hadn't he?

As a matter of fact, Virginia was having a very slight attack of conscience. She was wide awake and had nothing to do, since Susan, after a brief, drowsy eulogy on Gus, had gone straight to sleep. So she gave some thought to her poor father, who wanted to read and had no light, and at last got out of bed and unscrewed the lone bulb in their room.

She went quietly out into the hall and then paused. It was dark, so dark that she could see nothing at all, and she stretched out a tentative hand. She took an uncertain step forward, and as she did so, a white figure loomed up beside her.

Virginia dropped the bulb and would have screamed if her throat had not closed up.

"Stay where you are," Jim's voice said. "I think you've broken something."

Virginia felt a surge of fury, which was purely reaction from shock.

"You don't say!" she muttered through clenched teeth. "What shall I do? Stand here until the dawn breaks?"

"No. My feet are bare, but for you I'll risk them. I'll make my way back to my room and get something to sweep up the pieces."

"I'll get it," Virginia said. "You'd better not move. I'm wearing slippers. We Grahams always wear slippers. It's part of the gracious living to which we are reared."

"Oh, very well," Jim agreed. "Of course we Okies get toughened, but I suppose the appendix which I'm due to remove tomorrow morning will come out more smoothly if I don't have bits of glass sticking into the soles of my feet while I'm operating."

Virginia was moving away, but she called back, "I'm not so sure. At least it would keep you awake."

She presently returned with a flashlight, a newspaper, and a whisk broom. She began to sweep the glass vigorously onto the newspaper, and since Jim's feet were surrounded by fragments, she took pleasure in sweeping his bare toes with great gusto.

"I admire your efficiency," he said mildly, "but don't you think it would have been less painful if I had just walked on the glass?"

"Possibly. But this way there will be no after effects."

"What were you doing, anyway?" he asked after a moment.

"Actually it isn't any of your business, is it?"

"No. But what were you doing?"

"What were you doing?" Virginia countered.

"Well, it's that fellow, you know, the one I have sleeping in my office."

"I didn't know."

"He's a friend of mine," Jim explained. "No roof over his head and can't get one, so I let him sleep in the office. But if any urgent calls come in, he must get up, dress, fly over here, and throw pebbles against my window. I told him which window it was, but to err is only human, and when I heard a tapping against the bathroom window, I thought I'd better investigate. However, it turned out to be the branch of a tree."

"It seems a high rent to have to pay," Virginia said of the office dweller. "Listen, how about giving me the bulb out of your room, since you broke this one?"

"I broke it?"

"Of course you broke it. I wouldn't have dropped it if you hadn't loomed up beside me like a ghost. Don't you ever wear a robe over your pajamas?"

"I have a robe," he admitted. "A Christmas gift, but too handsome to wear. Anyway, don't you feel like Romeo and Juliet, standing here in the dark, conversing in low tones, in our nighties? Our families would have much to say, and all of it nasty, if they knew."

"Very funny," Virginia said, turning away. "I believe you're supposed to drink poison, aren't you? After which I end it all with a dagger. If I can't find just the right dagger, I don't think I'll bother, but don't let me stop you."

"I wasn't being funny," Jim called after her. "Remember, in school, when I started casting sheep's eyes at you and before you had a chance to spurn me, my mother forced me to stop by cutting off my Saturday movies until I did?"

Virginia paused by her door and asked coldly, "Oh, is that what happened?"

"Yes. I knew you always resented that so I'm explaining now, to clear things up between us."

"Oh, no, the fog's thicker than ever. I don't want a cheap love like that. I won't play second fiddle to the movies. Good night, Romeo."

She went into her room and closed the door, and Jim lit a cigarette and made his way back to bed.

Aloysius unglued his ear from the door of his room and stumbled to his bed in the dark. He was well satisfied with Virginia. She'd stepped on that insect, all right. The last thing he wanted was to have her hook up with a Larson. She was a good, attractive, intelligent girl, and someday he'd find a suitable husband for her. He'd have to look around a bit.

Evidently she'd relented and had been bringing him a bulb, and that damned Larson rat had scared her into dropping it. So now he couldn't read, and he couldn't sleep, either. Of course he'd slept until eleven that morning. It was the first chance he'd had for a late morning in many a day. Elsie was one of these confounded early risers and had always swept him out of bed and out of her sun parlor as one of her first chores for the day. She probably did it just for spite.

The bedside lamp suddenly glowed into the darkness, and Aloysius started violently. He glanced fearfully around the empty room and then at the lamp, burning steadily and brightly on the bedside table. It was uncanny and frightening, and he'd better take the thing apart and try to fix it. It was a loose wire. It must be a loose wire.

He shook his head and reached for his book and did not hear the quiet footsteps of P.X. Smith following that dark figure up to the attic.

Aloysius had reached a most breathless point in his story when the light went out again. There was no fading or flickering. It simply went off as though someone had turned the switch.

He could not stand the darkness, even aside from his desire to finish the book, and he decided to go downstairs and get a bulb from the hall or the living room. He groped his way out and down the stairs, and after stumbling around for a while located the hall light and switched it on. He peered into the living room and was astonished to see that P.X. Smith apparently had not gone to bed, since he was sitting in an armchair. Aloysius spoke to him, but there was no reply, and he was conscious of a cold uneasiness that seemed to start in the pit of his stomach. P.X. was so very still, much too still. He forced himself into the living room and switched on one of the lamps with a shaking hand.

P.X. Smith's dead face, smashed and bloody, gazed blankly back at him.

CHAPTER 12

ALOYSIUS BACKED SLOWLY into the hall, where he stood for a moment, unable to move or even to yell. When his shocked, confused mind became a little more coherent, he knew that he must get help. Larson. He must get hold of Larson. There was a lunatic running around loose, and they'd have to do something.

He started up the stairs, but he could not make himself hurry. His legs were wobbly and he was panting. He felt as though he were in one of those nightmares where he could not run away from an implacably advancing horror, but could only crawl slowly.

He reached the top of the stairs and crept to Jim Larson's door, where he knocked feebly. There was no reply, and after a moment he turned the knob and went in.

"Jim!" he called in a hoarse whisper. "Wake up. Quickly!"

Jim stirred, turned over, and burrowed his head into the pillow, and Aloysius felt a sudden return of his self-possession. What sort of a doctor did the fellow think he was, when he did not spring instantly to attention for a night call? He went to the bed and shook his shoulder roughly, and Jim awoke with a start. He was half out of bed at once, and nearly knocked Aloysius over.

"What is it? What's the matter?"

"Be quiet, will you!" Aloysius whispered fiercely. "Something is going on here. There's been a bad accident. We'll have to get the police."

Jim gripped him by the arm and said quietly, "All right! Don't get excited. What's happened?"

"It's downstairs. Come on, for God's sake."

Jim reached for his trousers, but Aloysius jerked him away and pushed him through the door. He was feeling more like himself every minute.

"It's that fellow, P.X. Smith. Somebody got him."

Jim, thoroughly awake now, recognized the shock and urgency in Aloysius's voice and made rapidly for the stairs without further ado. He called over his shoulder, "Whereabouts down here?"

"In the living room," Aloysius hissed back. "You can't miss it. It— it stares right at you."

They went down, and Aloysius realized, with sudden renewed terror, that the lights had been turned out again while he was upstairs. It was absolutely dark and still. He heard Jim make his way cautiously into the living room, and presently a light went on in there. Aloysius crept down the last two stairs and peered fearfully around the door.

P.X. Smith was no longer there.

Aloysius felt sick. Something horrible was going on. The man had been dead. He must have been dead. And, anyway, you couldn't walk around with your face practically gone.

"Looks as though you'd had a nightmare," Jim said into the silence.

Aloysius pulled himself together and sputtered angrily, "Nightmares be damned! I was as wide awake as you are now. I tell you he was sitting there, dead, with his face smashed in. And anyway, where is he? You'll have to admit that he's disappeared."

Jim made a cursory search of the room and the terrace outside, with Aloysius so close behind him that he twice trod on his heels.

"His bag has gone too," Jim said finally. "He's left, that's all. Probably didn't like it here and had another place to go with a better bed." To Aloysius's horror, he switched off the light and headed for the stairs.

"Wait a minute. You can't just go back to bed. We'll have to find him. I tell you he was sitting there in that chair and his face was all smashed and bloody."

Jim was halfway up the stairs. "I expect you were walking in your sleep and you didn't wake up until you came to my room. It's nothing to worry about, plenty of people are afflicted that way. I thought myself that the stew was a bit rich."

Aloysius, still following closely behind, felt utterly frustrated. He knew what he'd seen well enough, and there was no nightmare about it. But doctors were all the same. They wouldn't listen to a word you said. And if you did, in desperation, shout your symptoms at them, they sat back and twiddled a pencil with a faraway look in their eyes because they'd already made up their minds what was wrong with you, and they didn't want any interference. See you dead first.

When Jim reached his door, he turned with his hand on the knob. "Even if it's as you say what can we do about it? We've searched, and can't find him, and we have no phone here. If you want to take a walk to the police station and tell them about it, go ahead, but I have to operate in the morning, and I need my sleep."

He went into his room, said, "Good night," and closed the door firmly.

"In your hat," Aloysius muttered, groping his way back to his room. "What's good about it?"

He stubbed his toe sharply on his own bed and fell to raging inwardly. He'd go out, tomorrow, and buy all the light bulbs in town and stack them here in his own room and the other three would have to crawl to him before he'd let them have so much as a twenty-watt.

He went over to the bedside lamp and slapped it lightly. He turned the switch several times, and tried to screw the bulb more tightly, but found that it was already quite firm. It was no use. That lamp would light up when it happened to feel like it or when Oliver P.'s ghostly hand turned the switch.

After scaring himself into a sweat with this thought, he got into bed in a hurry.

But he could not sleep. He kept seeing P.X. Smith with that dreadful, mutilated face, and his mind revolved ceaselessly around the question of his present whereabouts. Someone had carried him out of the living room, and then what? Maybe the body was right here in this room with him now. He hadn't been able to search. It was too dark, and Oliver P. wouldn't turn the bedside light on.

Aloysius came out in a cold sweat all over his body, and he frantically told himself not to be a fool and to stop letting his imagination run away with him.

Not far away, in the main part of the house, Ed Randall was also putting in a restless night. It was the stairs that bothered him, people walking up or downstairs all night long, every time he dozed off. He reflected, uneasily, that he had never liked the Graham mansion, anyway. The place gave him the creeps. First, it was too elegant for him. Those finger bowls on lace doilies with a posy floating in the water, and Wister always at his elbow to do things for him that he could perfectly well do for himself, and Una got up in such a mess of lace, silk, and perfume that he was half afraid to touch her for fear he'd do some damage. And then that old bastard Oliver P. always jumping on his neck about something every time he came into the house.

Right now the old barn had the feeling of ghosts about it. Ghosts always walked up and down stairs. Ed laughed feebly to himself, turned over, and tried to go to sleep.

At six o'clock he gave up and got dressed. He couldn't sleep, and there was no use rolling around on Maude's fancy sheet any longer. He dressed carefully, put on his best tie with a view to showing Una what she had lost, and then decided to go out into the garden and pick a flower for his buttonhole.

He was halfway down the stairs before he realized that they were so heavily carpeted that you could not have heard a troop of soldiers mounting or descending them.

CHAPTER 13

ED LOOKED AT THE thickly carpeted stairs for a while with a puzzled frown and then turned suddenly and slapped at the wall beside him. It gave back a hollow sound, and he grinned as the perplexity died out of his face. The left wing, of course—old Oliver P.'s hangout. Those stairs were just on the other side of the wall and people were using them during the night. Ed's grin broadened, and he wondered whether the girls were doing a little moonshining. Or perhaps it was old Oliver P.'s ghost wandering around. He'd get Maude to change his room and give him a quieter one.

He went out to the back terrace and discovered that it was a glorious day, and his spirits lifted. He picked a few pansies and found one that he thought had a face like Bert's, which gave him a quiet laugh. After he had inspected a few more posies, he wandered back to the terrace and tried to peer in through the windows of the left wing, but he could not see much. As he stood there, an appetizing smell of bacon floated past him, and he realized that he was sharply hungry. He abandoned the left wing and walked briskly to the kitchen door, feeling pleased that the girls were up and had started breakfast so early. He opened the door and then stopped short. The kitchen was silent and empty, and the bacon smell had disappeared.

Ed felt a few goose-pimples prick out on his skin. He hesitated and then made his way back to the left wing, where he peered into the windows, one by one, until he caught sight of Susan and Jim cooking breakfast behind the bar. He chuckled then and went around to the French doors of the living room. He knew Jim, and he supposed that the Grahams had rented the wing to Jim and, presumably, his bride, who appeared to be a pretty girl with brown curls and blue eyes.

Ed burst in through the French doors and yelled, "Jim, you old pill slinger!"

Susan dropped a dish, and Jim, after a startled glance, relaxed into a smile. "Hello, Mr. Randall. Where did you blow in from?"

"I was stuck for a room, so I drove over and put up with the girls. They didn't tell me they'd rented out the left wing. What have you done with the old man's ghost? Shoved it into a closet?"

"Oh, hush!" Susan cried, and Jim, reminded of her, introduced her. Ed was glad he had put on his best tie when he discovered that she and Jim were not married. He exhibited as much glamour as his forty-eight years would allow and gave her a charming bow.

Susan was impressed to the point of forgetting Gus for a while, and she turned on some glamour of her own. They conversed prettily for a few minutes, until Ed began to wonder whether it was fair of him to edge in on Jim's girl this way. He looked around, and discovered that Jim now had another girl. He whistled and, as usual, spoke before thinking.

"You running a harem here, Jimmy?"

Jim, busy with bacon and coffee making, shook his head. "You're off the beam, Ed. You'd better listen carefully while I explain all."

He introduced Virginia and told the whole story, and by the time Ed had finished laughing, they were all, including himself, seated at the bar, eating breakfast.

"Little Virginia Graham," Ed said, chewing bacon with vim, "grown up, and beautiful as well. And the last time I saw you—"

"I was only a little girl."

"That's right. But where's your old man? Used to have some swell times with old Wishy." He caught Susan's eye and added hastily, "Of course he was a lot older than the rest of us fellows, but anyway, we had some swell times. Good old Wishy. Never shall I forget when they threw him out of—"

"I hope you won't give us away," Virginia said quickly. "We'll all be badly stuck if we have to move out of here."

"Not me. I wouldn't say a word. How long have you been here?"

"Just a couple of days," Susan told him.

"Well," Ed said judicially, "I don't know exactly what the legal aspect of the matter is, but so long as you're in, I think they'd have trouble evicting you."

Virginia shook her head. "That sounds all right, but somehow I think if they really want to evict us, we'll be out within an hour."

"Well, I know a man—" Ed began, but wasn't able to get anywhere in telling about his man, because everyone else knew a man, also, and couldn't be bothered hearing about Ed's. He persisted for a while, but when he found that he was definitely talking to himself, he gave up.

They washed up the dishes, and Jim said that they'd have to get some cutlery before evening and return what they had borrowed. In fact, when it had been washed and dried, they put it into Ed's pocket and gave him detailed instructions about the drawer into which it was to be replaced in the main kitchen.

Ed assured them that he'd take care of it and asked again after Aloysius. They told him where Aloysius was to be found, and after they had left, Ed went up and banged on the door of the master bedroom.

Aloysius woke up at once and got out of bed in a fury. He had made up his mind to sleep himself out every morning, and he muttered that he was going to kill the next person who came pounding outside his room. He flung the door wide, and Ed came breezing in and slapped him on the back.

As soon as Aloysius had got his breath, he yelled, "Good God, Ed! Don't tell me you're going to live here too. We won't be able to keep you quiet enough."

"Nah," said Ed. "I'm in the star bedroom over there as an honored guest."

"That's you all over," Aloysius said, half admiring and half annoyed. "Here, wait till I get my pants on, and we'll go down and have some breakfast."

Later, as they were going down the uncarpeted stairs, Ed asked, "What do you fellers do all night, going up and down these stairs? My room's close by here, and I'm telling you, boy, the traffic was heavy."

Aloysius, suddenly reminded of P.X. Smith, felt sick. He knew he hadn't had any nightmare. He had really seen that dreadful, battered face. And he knew he ought to do something about it, but he could not think of anything that would not result in his eviction. After all, when a person was dead, you could no longer help him, and he didn't want to be evicted.

He prepared some breakfast, and Ed waited with undiminished appetite to sit down with him. At the last minute, when everything vas ready, Aloysius could not find the cutlery, and it was not until he had cursed vigorously for some time that he caught sight of it sticking out of Ed's pocket.

He snatched it out and asked indignantly, "What do you think you're doing, anyway? This isn't a hotel."

"God's sake," Ed said aggrievedly. "I was asked to take them back to the kitchen by your own daughter. And I have never taken more than one piece at a time from any hotel."

They were in the midst of a hearty breakfast when Jim Larson appeared quietly at the French doors. He came in slowly and asked, "Up already, Mr. Graham?"

Aloysius looked at him warily without replying as Jim walked over to the armchair in which P.X. Smith had been sitting with his shattered face. Jim made no further comment, but stooped and began to examine the chair carefully.

"What goes on?" Ed asked, his fork suspended halfway between the plate and his mouth.

Aloysius left his breakfast and, joining Jim at the chair, began to examine the floor around it.

"For God's sake!" Ed exploded. "What are you looking for?"

Aloysius drew a long breath and said flatly, "Blood."

CHAPTER 14

ED GOT SLOWLY to his feet, looking from one to the other of them, and asked uneasily, "What sort of a nuthouse is this?"

Jim gave Aloysius a glance of contempt and said to Ed, "It's all right. Don't get excited. One of the girls cut her finger yesterday and bled on this chair, and we want to find it to clean it up."

Ed looked him over coldly. "So you come all the way back here in the middle of a busy morning to do some housework. Head for the shore, brother. That ice is too thin."

"God's sake!" Aloysius said in utter disgust. "Of all the silly, fishy, asinine stories I ever heard, that one is it. You think Ed is feeble-minded, or what?"

"If you'd kept your big fat mouth shut," Jim declared hotly, "we could have said we'd lost a valuable cufflink or something."

"Listen, fellers," Ed said pacifically. "Cut it out, will you, and tell me what this is all about."

Jim straightened up and shook his head. "As far as I can make out, old Sitting Bull there had a nightmare. There's no sign of blood, and if his story is true, there'd have to be some trace of it."

Aloysius turned his back on Jim and told Ed the whole story with dramatic gestures while Jim went back to inspecting the chair. It was upholstered in a dark red material, and he realized that any spot would look much the same, whether it were blood or lemonade. He could not find anything on the chair, but on the floor beside it he discovered a patch that stood out from the dusty surrounding area because it had been wiped clean. He looked at it for a while, frowning, and then straightened abruptly and walked toward the French doors.

Ed called after him, but he replied shortly that he had not found anything and went on. He felt irritated and annoyed about that cleaned spot, because it gave some substance to Aloysius's wild story, and he had fervently hoped that the whole thing had been a nightmare.

He walked to his office, where he found Susan conversing earnestly with a young man who was clad only in pajamas and who yawned sleepily at intervals.

Jim lost what little temper he had left. "You pick up your things and get out of here," he roared. "I gave you plenty of warning about getting out in the morning, and look at you!"

The young man grabbed up some clothes as he was run out and eventually put them on in the hall. After he had gone, Jim attempted to relieve the rest of his bad temper on Susan, but she told him, amiably, to go and boil his head. In the end, he spent his emotions on a patient in the hospital whom he caught smoking a big black cigar which had been smuggled in to him. When Jim had finished with him, he was pale green and immediately sent for his lawyer to make his will.

Gus called for Susan at lunch time, and she sneaked out a little early, leaving one or two of her chores for Jim to do. Jim cleaned up the odds and ends when he came in and then went along to the Kuntree Koffee Shoppe to wait for Virginia. He had decided that Aloysius would be tied up with Ed, since they were kindred souls, and would not show up.

Virginia came in looking distinctly cross, which put Jim in a better humor at once. He led her to a table, with a good deal of manner, but all she said was, "What are you doing here?"

Jim looked suitably astonished. "We had a date for lunch."

"No. That was yesterday. Father and Dr. Hanson horned in, remember? And you had to pay for everybody."

Jim nodded. "Bert was a little upset at my getting stuck, but I told him that since I was stuck for you and your father, I might as well be stuck with him as well. He thought that was a huge joke and let me pay."

"Didn't it occur to Bert that he was stuck along with you?"

"No," said Jim, "that never occurred to him."

Virginia picked up the menu. "Listen, what are you doing here?"

Jim became more serious and, fingering the cutlery abstractedly, told her about Aloysius and his story of P.X. Smith.

"If your father merely imagined the whole thing," he finished, "there's something wrong with him and he needs medical attention. If he didn't, then we should notify the police, and we'll certainly be evicted."

Virginia looked at him with scared gray eyes and wished despairingly that she and her father had never left Aunt Elsie's sun parlor. But it was too late now, they couldn't go back. Aunt Elsie had cleared it out, prepared to use it herself, only to find another relative installed there.

Jim had been watching her and he said now, "I thought I'd better tell you because Susan would only scream.'"

"Maybe she would," Virginia said perversely, "but that just happens to be the way she reacts to some things. She can think as well as you or anyone."

"Did I say she couldn't think?" Jim demanded. "She thinks all the time, around in circles. I said she would scream, and I still say so, and furthermore, she'd tell everyone in sight. But something has to be done, and I think if you'll help me, perhaps we can find out what happened to that man, and we can postpone reporting it, at least for a while."

"Aren't you forgetting that I'm a Graham?" Virginia asked acidly.

"Certainly not. It's merely a matter of expediency, anyway. I need help, and you are the best of three possibilities."

"You can call me a possibility," Virginia said coldly, "but what you mean is that you need an errand boy."

"Oh, forget the damned feud for a while," he replied, suddenly impatient. "This is serious."

Virginia dropped her troubled eyes and frowned down at the table.

"I know. But I don't see what you can do about it. You've no training for that sort of an investigation, and neither have I."

"Can't you give me a chance? And some help? Where the devil are we all going to live if we get kicked out of there? But we'll have to do something about Smith—we can't just drop it."

"No," she sighed. "There's something queer about Maude and Una, anyway. They were always frightful spendthrifts, you know, and their father was, too. He lost a lot of money in some foolish speculations just before he died and I don't think there was much left. But the girls have the insurance, which was left in the form of an annuity and comes to about a thousand a month. You'd think they could live comfortably on that."

"You would think so," Jim agreed. "Of course that's an expensive place to keep up."

She nodded. "But they're running it for way under a thousand a month. No servants, no clothes, no entertaining nor any activities. They practically live on nuts and berries from the garden, and it would never surprise me to hear that Maude goes out at night and shoots rabbits for stew. Wister gets something to eat at his nightclub, and I have a suspicion that he brings scraps home, too. They try to make out that he's still their butler. In fact, they try desperately to maintain that they're not poverty-stricken when it's quite obvious that they are."

"Wister has plenty of money," Jim said thoughtfully. "I saw him counting it."

Virginia looked up at him, and her eyes widened. "Why, that's what it is, Jim! Blackmail. We'll have to catch him at it and expose him."

She stood up, full of excitement and purpose and, catching up the check, began to rummage in her purse.

Jim took the check away from her and handed it to the waitress with a bill.

"The new world is not yet come," he said austerely. "I still attend to the financial details when lunching out with a lady."

"You paid yesterday," Virginia protested, "and as one worker to another, I maintain that it's my turn."

Jim pocketed his change and steered her toward the door. "The Larsons are chivalrous to infinity—infinity, for them, being the point where they have to pay for a Graham's lunch. But I am true to my training, so you may as well drop the subject."

They had emerged onto the sidewalk and they were both brought up short by the sight of Wister, hanging on to a lamppost and obviously dead drunk.

CHAPTER 15

VIRGINIA AND JIM stood for a moment, held immobile by their own surprise. Wister had always been the embodiment of discretion, his conduct above reproach, and neither of them could remember having seen him take a drink in all the years they had known him.

Jim went over, at last, and tried to straighten the dangling figure. "Come on, Wister—you'd better go home."

Wister tried, briefly, to focus his eyes, and gave it up immediately. He began to sing snatches of "Ta Ra Ra Boom De Ay."

Jim glanced over his shoulder at Virginia and handed her his key ring. "Bring my car around here, will you? I'm going to take him home."

Virginia took the keys and hurried off. She located the car on a side street. It was newly painted a shining cream color but rather ancient as to engine. She had a little trouble starting it, and when at last she managed to get it going, it sounded like a motorcycle. She presently drew up alongside Jim and Wister, where an unexpected difficulty presented itself. Wister refused to enter the car.

"I am a retainer, shir—sir. More fitting for me to walk."

"Not this time," Jim said firmly. "You couldn't make it. Come on, drop the lamppost, will you?"

There was a prolonged scuffle, which eventually ended in Wister being deposited, like a sack of stubborn potatoes, in the back seat.

"Drive to the Graham place," Jim said to Virginia, breathing hard.

"But I'll be late back at the office, even now."

"The office will stagger along," Jim said peevishly. "I'll give you a doctor's certificate to say you had a hangover."

Virginia engaged the gear with a loud grinding noise and the car started with a vicious jerk. "You're not my doctor," she pointed out nastily.

Jim grunted. "Don't tell me you get Bertram Hanson to hand out your pills for you."

Virginia ground the gears again but said nothing. Wister gave a high, thin laugh.

"She calls me an old maid but there's an old maid for you—Bert Hanson. I've known him for yearsh—years and years and yearsh. He'd keep a tabby if it could get along without eating but food costs money. Looked under his bed every night for thirty years, and never yet found anything but the chamber pot—" He stopped suddenly and glanced at Virginia. "Beg pardon, mish—I thought you had left some time ago."

Virginia steered for a hole and bounced the car over it. Jim leaned back against the seat, laughing.

"Who called you an old maid, Wister? You're nothing of the sort. They're just jealous."

"Ah, jealous—yes. Very jealous—too jealous." He was suddenly asleep, with his head on Jim's shoulder, and he remained drowsy while Jim helped him to his room, undressed him, and put him to bed.

When Jim emerged from Wister's room, he found Virginia and Maude having coffee at the kitchen table. Maude immediately invited him to have a cup and, after a moment's hesitation, he sat down. He glanced at his watch and murmured, "I haven't much time," as Maude reached for the percolator.

"Ah, come off it," Virginia muttered. "You've time to burn. You had a patient today. You wouldn't expect to get any more."

"On the contrary," Jim said with dignity, "they are probably hanging on the chandeliers in my waiting room at this moment."

"Listen, stop the vaudeville cross talk," Maude interposed. "Tell me about. Wister. What is the matter with him? He never touched a drop in his life, so I don't see how he can be drunk."

"He is definitely inebriated, madam," Jim said, and Virginia choked over her coffee.

"Don't you 'madam' me, Jim Larson," Maude said tartly. "If Wister is drunk, then he has had a bad shock of some sort. Either that or somebody fooled him."

Jim frowned thoughtfully down at his coffee. "He had quite a large sum of money, of course. Perhaps he lost it, or it was stolen."

Maude looked up at him. "Money? I suppose that might explain it. He always stumbled over his feet getting to the bank with money, for fear it might be lost on the way. But he always put it in in driblets. He couldn't have had much."

"He had a sizable roll of hundred-dollar bills."

Maude shook her head. "No, they were ones. Tips, probably."

"They were not ones," Jim said positively.

Virginia stirred and sighed. "I'll have to get back to the office before they report me to Missing Persons."

"Don't go back, dear," Maude suggested comfortably. "Phone and tell them you're sick."

"Well—" Virginia sighed again and then laughed. "That's both of you. I think I'll break down and do it, only I shan't say I'm sick. I'll merely give a few directions over the phone about what I want done with my work."

She stood up and went through to the hall, and Maude looked after her with frank admiration. "Whoever would have thought that Aloysius' girl would be so attractive?"

"She didn't show much promise when she was a kid," Jim admitted. "Thin and puny, hair hanging in strings, and her face and hands always dirty."

Maude nodded. "That was Aloysius. He always considered it more important to stuff her with ice-cream cones and take her to the movies than to clean her up. He and Father had a tremendous row about it. Father believed himself to be thoroughly experienced in bringing up girls, and he wanted to show Aloysius what to do at every turn. But Wishus must have been right, after all, and Father wrong, because Virginia is completely dependable and worthwhile, and Una and I are shiftless derelicts."

"What absurd nonsense," Jim said, smiling lazily at her.

"No, it isn't, really." She laughed a little and added, "Certainly it was absurd for Father and Aloysius to quarrel over such a thing. They had not spoken to each other for ten years when Father died."

"I never knew that," Jim said in some surprise.

Maude nodded. "Father gave up referring to Wishus by name altogether. Always called him 'that blasted idiot.'"

Virginia came back into the kitchen, looking relieved and satisfied. "Well, that's that. Now I think I'll go home and attend to several things that have to be attended to."

"I'll drive you back," Jim said, getting to his feet. "I have to go, anyway. Office hours."

Maude went to the door with them and then wandered through to the back of the house rather aimlessly. She heard Una and Ed talking and laughing together, and saw through one of the French doors in the dining room that they were sitting on the lawn. Bert would have a fit if he could see them, she thought, and shrugged indifferently. Bert was a miserable specimen, and Una would do much better to go back to Ed. But she felt a spasm of pity for Bert. After all, he had always been good to them, and she knew that Una would jilt him without a moment's hesitation if she did decide that she wanted Ed again. Oh, well, better stay out of it entirely and let Una mess up her own life.

Her main concern now was to track down the old man who had startled Una and find out whether it was Father or not. If she could only get hold of him, face to face, she'd have it out with him and come to some reasonable agreement. Probably, though, it was just Una's imagination. She herself had spent a lot of time hanging around the hotel and the town, but she hadn't seen him. He'd collected the money and gone, maybe, although it was pretty daring to come for it himself. Anyway, she'd gone up to the attic in Father's wing and made sure that the money was gone, and there was nothing else she could do, at least for a while. Next month, when they put the money there, she was going to hide and then follow whoever collected it. She'd find out where Father was then and confront him. They might all land in jail, but even that would be a change from this lousy state of affairs.

She went into the cool dimness of the library and stretched out on a couch. A little sleep wouldn't hurt her tired mind and body.

She was awakened, some time later, by Una pulling frantically at her shoulder. She jerked away irritably and then woke up completely as she saw the fear in Una's smoky gray eyes.

"The money!" Una wailed. "Something happened! It's been stolen. Father never got it."

CHAPTER 16

MAUDE SAT UP, her mind instantly alert. "Father never got that money?"

"No, no, he didn't. Of course I said we'd left it there, as usual."

"You put it there yourself, didn't you?"

"Of course I put it there!" Una cried indignantly. "Are you insinuating that I kept it?"

"Don't be an ass," Maude said mildly. "Not that I'd blame you if you did." She sighed, yawned, and rubbed a closed fist across her forehead. "I suppose it was stolen."

"Yes, but what are we going to do? Where can we raise a thousand dollars right away?"

Maude got off the couch, adjusted the shoulder straps of her brassiere, pulled down her girdle, and said decisively, "We're not going to try. We left the damn money there, and if someone has stolen it, it's just his hard luck. Evidently someone has found out about it, and we'll have to change the hiding place."

"Oh, Maude, he'll do something dreadful. He'll expose us. Why did we ever agree to all this in the first place? We should have known—" Una's voice trailed off into dreary sobbing.

Maude hardly noticed her. She was thinking, suddenly, of Wister, and Jim Larson's story that he had had a roll of hundred-dollar bills. That must be it. Wister had found out about it and had taken the money, not to steal, for Wister would never steal anything, but with some idea in his head of protecting them.

"Wister," she said out loud.

Una stopped sobbing and asked, "What?"

"Wister has it. We'll go and talk to him."

"Maude, are you out of your mind?" Una cried wildly. "You can't say anything to Wister. You'll hurt his feelings terribly. You know perfectly well that he wouldn't touch any money except his own."

"I know all that," Maude agreed, making for the kitchen. "I'm not going to accuse him. I merely want to ask him why."

Una pattered along behind, saying agitatedly, "No, no, you can't.

This is awful. Wister wouldn't dream of such a thing. What makes you think he has it?"

She hung back in the kitchen while Maude went straight into Wister's room and shook him vigorously by the shoulder. He opened one unseeing eye and then closed it again, and although Maude persisted for several minutes, she was unable to get any further reaction from him. She returned to the kitchen, frowning, and muttered, "Damn it, I'll have to wait until he gets over it."

"What is it? What's wrong with him?" Una asked.

"Drunk," said Maude briefly. "Dead to the world."

"Oh, not—" Una twisted her hands together and whispered, "Not Wister."

"Yes, he is. Brought home drunk by Dr. J. Larson, diagnosed, politely, as inebriated by said J. Larson, and you can believe me when I say that he's boiled."

Una turned away and began to cry, and Maude stared at her in some perplexity.

"What is it now?" she demanded after a moment. "Why the devil have you taken to spilling tears all over the house from morning till night? And what the hell is it to you if Wister is drunk, except funny?"

Una mopped rather hurriedly at her eyes and said in a strained voice, "Why, nothing. Nothing at all. It's just that everything has been so awful, and then Wister getting drunk, of all things, simply seemed the last straw. But it doesn't mean anything to me, naturally."

She began to carry the cups that Maude, Virginia, and Jim had used earlier to the sink, with her face half averted.

Maude stood where she was without moving and became conscious of a faintly sick feeling at the pit of her stomach. So that was it. Una, she knew, had always been boy-crazy, but Wister! And yet it was not the first time that Una had shocked her in this way. Still, Wister! Oh well, what was so wrong with Wister, anyway? He was decent and honest to the core. What was wrong with Una was more like it. If she were fooling around with Wister, then it was just an interlude, because she would never be really serious about him. People might laugh and Una was very vain. No, she'd throw Wister to one side when she married Bert.

But Una seemed a bit afraid of Wister. She had fainted when he had appeared from his room and asked them to be more quiet. Perhaps she had thought that he was going to expose her philandering at that time. And then, when he had overheard Una becoming engaged to Bert, he had gone out and got drunk. She shivered a little and thought perhaps she only imagined the whole thing. But still, she always had wondered why Wister hung on.

Una wiped some crumbs from the table onto the floor and asked querulously, "Why are you standing there dreaming? For heaven's sake, go on up and get dressed. You know Bert's having us for dinner tonight and it will be promptly at six, as usual."

"Oh God!" Maude groaned. "I'd forgotten. I hate eating dinner in the middle of the afternoon, especially when there's no chance of cocktails. Since it's us, he'll stretch a point and bring out the cooking sherry. Can't we take Ed along?"

"You know perfectly well we can't. Do go and get dressed."

Maude went dejectedly out of the kitchen, wondering if there were anything in the world that bored her more than going to dinner at Bert's, and Una followed, looking scarcely more cheerful. She could put up with the dinner, she thought—after all, it wouldn't last forever—but she was frightened all the time now. How had she gotten into so much trouble, anyway? It seemed to be pressing in on her from all sides. Ed was amusing, but she couldn't stand living with him. You never knew where you were. Sometimes he came home for dinner and sometimes he didn't, but he always had a voluble excuse. And sometimes there was money and sometimes none at all. No. With Bert, there would always be money, and she'd be able to get some of it out of him.

She began to mount the stairs, and Ed caught her halfway up.

"Hi, there, sugar, what are you doing tonight?"

Una told him, and he looked pained. "You mean I have to eat by myself?"

"Have you ever," Una asked, "eaten by yourself in your whole life? I doubt it."

She went on upstairs, and Ed sent a grin after her and then considered, whistling softly through his teeth. He might as well join Wishy's crowd. Two damn good-looking girls, and Wishy was and always had been one of the boys. There was never a dull moment when

Wishy was around.. He went down again, laughing to himself at all that activity going on in the left wing with Maude and Una none the wiser. He went through the dining room, out onto the terrace, and advanced into the flower garden, where he was brought to a sudden chilling stop.

Virginia and Jim, each with a shovel, had uprooted an entire petunia bed and were digging grimly in the soft earth.

Ed approached slowly, running a nervous hand over his head, because his scalp prickled. "Look, you two, don't you think you're carrying this thing a bit too far? If that old man had been killed—if he were missing—surely there'd be someone inquiring for him."

Jim leaned on his shovel and wiped his perspiring forehead. "He said he was up here on business and that he hadn't completed it, so I don't suppose anyone would start hunting for him yet. I still think Aloysius was dreaming, but I'd like to make sure."

"Well, now, look," Ed said reasonably. "You know Wishy—best feller in the world—but nobody can deny that he mops it up sometimes, and when he's like that, he sees anything he feels like seeing."

Jim nodded. "I'm more than half convinced that that's the explanation, but still—"

"You both talk," Virginia interposed coldly, "as though Father were an alcoholic. I suppose he drinks less in a year than you two guzzle in a week. After all, he only drinks to be sociable."

"You might call it that," Ed admitted with a reminiscent grin.

Jim bent to his shovel again, and Ed presently asked uneasily, "What do you expect to find, anyway?"

"Well, if he was killed, someone hid the body. It isn't in our part of the house—we've searched thoroughly—and these beds are full of loose earth. It wouldn't take too long to bury him in one of them."

Virginia turned her head away and Jim glanced at her. "Why don't you go back to the house? This is no job for you. It's been too much for you, anyway—searching the wing, and all that. Give Ed your shovel. He can help me."

Ed backed away a step and felt himself shiver from head to foot. He wasn't going to poke around, looking for what they expected to find.

Virginia straightened up and said through her teeth, "Don't be ridiculous, Larson—I can do this as well as you." She shifted over to an adjoining bed, which was the beginning of the vegetable garden, and began to dig furiously among some tenderly sprouting tomato, plants that Maude had fondly hoped would grow up and save some money for her.

Virginia flung clods of earth right and left, and then, quite suddenly, she stood absolutely still, and the shovel fell from her hand. She dropped quietly to the ground before Jim could catch her, and with one hand groping for her, he turned and looked into the hole she had made.

P.X. Smith's black goatee lay there, unattached to anything and dirt-matted, but still shapely.

CHAPTER 17

ED RUSHED OVER and knelt by Virginia. He raised her head on his arm and cried excitedly, "What's the matter with her? What's happened? Quick, Jim, for God's sake do something."

"She's only fainted," Jim said abstractedly, still peering into the hole. "Put her head down and leave her alone."

Ed backed away and asked wildly, "Can't you do something for her? This is awful."

Jim left the hole rather reluctantly and turned his attention to Virginia, and Ed, relieved on that score, went over to see what had caused all the excitement. He drew in his breath sharply when he saw the goatee and stretched a tentative hand, but Jim's voice, behind him, said peremptorily, "Leave it alone."

Ed left it alone. He straightened up, lit a cigarette, and burned his fingers on the match.

Virginia stirred and opened her eyes. Jim spoke to her in a low voice while Ed came and crouched beside her awkwardly, anxious to help but having no idea what to do. Jim moved away and gingerly picked up the small tuft of matted hair. There were flecks of blood on it and the end had been cut straight and even, as though with a pair of scissors. He pulled out a handkerchief, the one he kept in his breast pocket for show, and wrapped the thing carefully.

Virginia spoke suddenly, and her voice was resentful. "Who hit me?"

"Nobody hit you, baby," Ed said eagerly. "You up and passed out all by your little self."

Jim put the handkerchief carefully into his pocket and said firmly, "You're going home, and you're going to bed. I told you to leave, just before you turned your toes up. I could see the whites of your eyes even then but you always know better than anyone else. Come on, Ed, give me a hand."

They raised her between them and began to walk her slowly toward the left wing. She was thoroughly mortified and protested irritably, "I can walk perfectly well by myself, if you'd only leave me alone." But she was relieved when they continued to support her because she felt a bit inclined to buckle at the knees.

"Why don't you take care of yourself?" Jim asked impatiently. "A little thing like that shouldn't make you keel over."

Virginia looked sulky and muttered, "We've been rushed at the office."

"And you've probably been getting too little sleep and reducing as well, just to help things along."

"I have not!" Virginia yelled. "I've never had to reduce in my life."

Arrived at the picket fence, they hoisted her over and took her into the living room, where she stopped suddenly.

"Where is it? That—that thing. Was it attached?"

"Attached!" Ed whispered hollowly.

Jim shook his head. "It had been cut off. I have it in my pocket."

"What are we going to do?"

"You're going to bed and you're going to stay there. You need rest."

"Shouldn't you hand me over to my own doctor?"

"Certainly," Jim agreed heartily. "I'll phone Bert right away and get him over here. You should never take chances with your health, even if it does mean that we'll all be thrown out."

"Ah, you talk too much," Virginia said as they moved on toward the stairs. "I can stand old Hanson occasionally but I don't believe I could put up with him when I'm not feeling well."

Ed chuckled. "If you ever want to spread anything all over the countryside, just tell it to Bert in confidence." He added, without venom, "The old washerwoman."

They took Virginia up to her room. She had a bit of a battle to push them out while she undressed. Their solicitude was such that she stripped off her clothes in record time and had barely slipped between the sheets when they barged in again. However, they did not stay for long. Jim put a finger on her pulse for a moment and then left, pushing Ed in front of him. He went downstairs, made a cup of tea, brushed some little red ants off a piece of cake, and took it up to her. Ed followed at his heels, but as soon as Virginia was established with pillows behind her back and the tray on her lap, Jim pushed him out again.

"We'll have to go back and see if we can find the rest of him," Jim said as they went down the stairs.

"I, er, think I have an appointment."

"You do for a fact," Jim agreed. "With a shovel. I don't want to do this alone."

Ed ran a finger around the inside of his collar and then pulled out a sizable handkerchief and wiped the moisture from his brow. But he followed along and when they arrived back at the vegetable garden, he picked up Virginia's shovel and began to dig in dogged silence.

Maude was in the kitchen, but she did not see them. She was waiting for Wister to come out of his stupor and was wandering aimlessly from stove to refrigerator to table. Except for a very recent layer of crumbs and coffee cups, the room was spotless. It was too close to Wister to be anything else.

Maude, chewing abstractedly on her thumb, opened the oven door, closed it, and stood staring blankly at the shining white surface. If Una had been fooling around with Wister, then she was almost embarrassed to face him. During the war there had been no single men of Una's age, not around these parts, anyway, except Bert. And Wister. Bert had flat feet, or something, and Wister a punctured eardrum.

She turned away from the stove abruptly and glanced at the door leading to the hall. Una was somewhere close by, prepared to listen, no doubt about that, but of course she wouldn't show herself.

She was almost ready to give up and postpone it when she heard sounds from Wister's room. He moved around quietly for some time, and then the door opened and he stood there looking at her.

She tackled him at once. "Wister, we have lost a considerable amount of money. We had it hidden in the left wing, in the attic. Do you know anything about it?"

He remained quite still, one hand on the doorknob, looking at her. His face was expressionless.

Maude heaved an exasperated little sigh. He so often did this when you asked him a direct question.

"Wister, for heaven's sake, either you do or you don't. Please answer me."

He let go of the doorknob and advanced a few steps into the kitchen.

"Miss Maude, in all the years that I have worked for your family and for you, I have never touched anything that was not mine."

"You know perfectly well that I'm not questioning your honesty," Maude said impatiently. "But it would be just like you to see it there and feel that you should put it in a safer place."

"I should not presume to do any such thing," he replied formally. "And now, miss, if you will excuse me, I must go. I am required to be at the café early this evening."

Maude turned away and stared out of the window, feeling cross and dissatisfied. He had not answered her, really, but she knew that she'd get nothing more out of him in this mood. She heard him say, "Good night, Miss Maude," as the back door closed behind him.

He's an antique, she thought irritably. His whole life spent in serving people, even at that wretched roadhouse. And although he still clung to it, his way of life was going out of fashion. People were serving themselves these days. But Wister seemed to love it, unless it was Una he loved and he could not face leaving her. It wouldn't be correct for the butler to love the daughter of the house. At least it wouldn't be correct to do anything about it. Had they? Or hadn't they?

She heard Una come in behind her and ask in a half whisper, "What did he say?"

"Nothing. And he said it very well, too."

They were both silent for a moment, and then Maude's eyes widened and she gasped.

"My garden! Una, look! My garden! It's all dug up!"

Una looked, but Maude was already out of the door and flying across the lawn. Jim and Ed did not hear her until she was close behind them and then she let out a yell that Ed, fearful of uncovering a dead body at any moment, was to dream about for months. He lost his head completely and to Maude's shrill demands for an explanation, offered the feeble story that he had lost a valuable cufflink.

"Don't talk rubbish like that to me, Ed Randall!" Maude cried, incensed. "Does a cufflink, valuable or cheap, have legs so that it could burrow itself into holes two feet deep? Try again."

"Wait a minute, Maude," Jim said quietly. "This is important. You can take my word for it. We'll restore the beds when we've finished, so calm down."

"Calm down be damned! Do you know how many dollars' worth of seed and how much work went into that garden? What am I to use for vegetables now?"

They both looked at her rather curiously and she realized that she'd made a mistake. Her temper died away, and she said rather flatly, "It's just that with food so short everywhere I hate to see it wasted. Always try not to waste any. What are you doing, anyway?"

"Well," Jim said evasively, "if you'll just be patient with us, we'll tell you very soon. Come on, Ed, we've finished here. No use digging any more."

He started off, and Ed trailed after him, looking back over his shoulder to say placatingly, "It's all right, Maudie, we'll fix it later." He saw Una approaching and hastily closed the gap between Jim and himself. He was in no condition to face either one of the girls, let alone the two of them together.

Jim took a long, circuitous route through the woods to reach the left wing, and when they arrived there, Ed was panting. He felt that never in his life had he needed a drink so badly.

Aloysius was cooking dinner and grumbling loudly to Susan.

"I can't do this every night, y'know, cooking for a lot of lazy, ungrateful clucks. I have my own life to live."

Susan fluttered around him, saying that she'd love to help, but he did not cheer up noticeably until Ed put a drink into his hand. He promised Ed the second choicest portion of the coming meal, having earmarked the best for Virginia and himself, and then turned to the other two and asked belligerently, "Where in hell is Virginia?"

"She's in bed," Jim told him briefly. "She isn't well. What's all the fuss about, anyway? Let me finish the cooking. I can do it in half the time."

"You keep your hands off," Aloysius said excitedly. "I'm hungry and I want a decent meal, not some Larson slop."

"You fix the cocktails, Jim," Ed suggested pacifically. "Wishy and I have had only one drink. We'll need a dividend."

Wishy gave Ed a narrow look and asked, "Don't those girls feed you, that you have to come here all the time?"

"Oh, sure, but they're going to Bert's for dinner and even if I'd been invited, I can't eat horsemeat, dog biscuits, and lemonade." He guffawed loudly, and when he found that no one was laughing with him, he added anxiously, "You don't mind, do you?"

Virginia came in wrapped in a dressing gown of palest lavender which seemed to put a hint of blue in her gray eyes and to make her pale hair almost silver. Susan, hovering solicitously, settled her into an armchair, and Jim handed the cocktails around.

Aloysius, suddenly cheerful, left dinner simmering on the grill and looked with a critical eye into the cold, faintly green depths of his dry martini. It seemed to satisfy him, for he held the frosted glass aloft and said genially, "Let's see. Who'll we drink to?"

"Why not to me?" asked a chilly voice from the hall.

They turned, as one person, to see Maude standing in the doorway.

CHAPTER 18

THERE WAS DEAD SILENCE as Maude advanced into the room. She looked at the dinner simmering on the grill and at the tray of cocktails, and her odd tawny eyes sparkled with fury. It was not so much the fact of these people being on her property that roused her anger as it was that she hated having been outsmarted by Aloysius.

She looked him straight in the eye and said curtly, "Explain yourself."

Aloysius glared back at her, his mind already busy with plans for revenge on somebody. "What sneaking rat told you we were here?"

"Nobody told me, you old fool. But with noise enough to wake the dead going on in a deserted wing of my house, it vaguely crossed my mind that I should investigate."

Aloysius turned to his companions in crime and said accusingly, "How many times did I tell you to be quiet?"

"But you told us in such a loud voice," Jim murmured.

"Just pack up and get out, all of you," Maude said with finality.

There was a brief silence, then Susan spoke up in a scared little treble. "I don't believe you can put us out, actually, Mrs. Watson. We are three veterans, and one of us's poor old father."

Aloysius frowned at her, puzzled as to who might be the poor old father. He wondered whether she could possibly be referring to P.X. Smith.

"I mean it," Susan went on, her voice gaining confidence. "My friend Gus says you can't evict much of anybody, and veterans, never. Jim Larson was a captain, you know, and I was a lieutenant in the Army Nurse Corps, and poor little Virginia, there—she isn't feeling so well tonight, which would make it worse, don't you think? Anyway, she was a private in the Marines. I mean, we'd only have to kick up a bit of a fuss, you see, and it would get into the newspapers and you'd surely be stoned, or something."

"You pack up and get out of here," said Maude furiously, "and then let them bring their stones. I've been wanting a rock garden for some time."

"Now, wait a minute, Maudie," Ed said nervously. "Why not let them stay? They've been here for a couple of days already, and you never even knew it."

Maude turned around on him. "You shut up, or I'll put you out too."

"We are willing to pay a good rent," Jim observed, apparently addressing the ceiling.

Maude swallowed twice before she was able to speak, but at last she said bravely, "Go and start your packing." She hated to think of all that money walking out of the house, but she could not back down at that point.

"Well," Aloysius said loudly, "I'm staying. You go ahead and call the cops, or whatever the procedure is. I'm not going till I'm thrown."

"You're not?" Maude asked softly.

"No. And you ought to be ashamed of yourself. These three young people are veterans."

"And you?"

"I'm the father of one of them, and why should a veteran be separated from its father?"

"Maude is quite right," Virginia said suddenly. "We haven't any business here, veterans or no, and we should never have come in the first place. I'm going upstairs now and pack my things. I'm leaving."

Aloysius turned on her with a wounded howl, and Jim said abruptly, "No." He stepped in front of Aloysius and said to Maude, "Virginia isn't well. I'm asking you to let us stay overnight, and I'll try to find somewhere for her and her father to go in the morning."

Maude glanced at Virginia and then shrugged. "Well, all right. But see that you make some other arrangement first thing in the morning."

She turned to leave, but Ed put a hand on her arm and pulled her back. "Don't go, Maudie, not with that long face on you. Stay and have a drink with us."

Maude hesitated. "I haven't time. Una and I are going to Bert's for dinner."

Ed nodded. "I know, I meant to write you a letter of condolence. But there's no harm in your getting oiled first. In fact, it's necessary. You know Bert—brown rubbing alcohol he calls sherry, served in liqueur glasses, and only one to a customer."

Maude grinned reluctantly, and her eye wandered to the clear, cold martinis in their frosted glasses. "All right," she said suddenly. "Don't forget the olive."

She had intended to have one and then go, but Jim had a way with cocktails, and she presently found herself halfway through the third. Susan was also into her third drink, while Aloysius and Ed had lost count. Virginia was not drinking and Jim sat with his first cocktail, practically untouched, in front of him.

He was thinking that he'd have to get in touch with the police.

There was no way out of it. It was a nasty business, and Maude would be furious. You couldn't blame her, either. They'd brought the old man there themselves, without her knowing anything about it. Oh, well, he'd attend to it immediately after dinner and get it over with. He wandered over to Virginia and sat down beside her.

"I think I'll have to tell Maude about Smith," he said in an undertone. "I'll have to go to the police, and she should hear about it first."

Virginia nodded on long sigh. "It's a mess. Poor old man. We'll have to find his family."

"It must have been a thief," Jim said, rumpling his hair, "and poor old Smith got in the way."

"Queer sort of thief to carry the body away, cut off the goatee, and then hide them in different places."

"I think the body and the goatee were both in that tomato bed," Jim said after a moment. "I don't know whether you noticed it, but the bed had been dug up before and the plants were wilting a little. Later the body was taken away to a better hiding place and the goatee forgotten. At least, that's the way it looks to me."

She nodded and then gave a little shiver. "Why was the goatee cut off in the first place? It—it seems so senseless."

Jim shrugged, and at the same moment Aloysius noticed them talking together and came over at once to break it up.

"Come on, honey, leave that raw Swede and join your old dad in a little drink."

Virginia shook her head. "I don't feel like drinking tonight or getting out of this chair, either. If you want to part us, get the raw Swede to move."

"All right, Larson," said Aloysius briskly. "You heard what the lady said."

"I am nonmoving," said Jim as he settled back comfortably. Aloysius made a few remarks, for which his daughter reprimanded him sharply, and then pulled up a chair and made it a threesome.

Una, coming down the stairs in a gray chiffon dinner dress and some good pearls, ready for and resigned to Bert's party, saw the open left-wing door and heard the sounds of revelry. She went through the door hastily and then stood at the entrance to the living room, her expression changing from amazement to indignation.

Maude and Susan were screaming with laughter at one of Ed's
jokes and they did not see her. She looked around the room and
noticed that Virginia was in a dressing gown. She also saw the saucepans on the grill, now giving forth a slightly burned odor.

Maude had rented the wing, she thought angrily, without telling
her a thing about it. And of course one of these tenants must have
stolen that money from the attic.

She stalked over and tapped Maude on the shoulder.

Maude was in high good humor by this time and to Una's accusa-
tions and recriminations she yelled hearty denials, calling loudly upon
the assembled company to back her up. Una said bitterly that she
would not believe any of them and Maude least of all. She sent a
dark, outraged look around and hung onto her pearls in a distinctly
insulting fashion.

Jim decided that it was as good a time as any to break the news
about P.X. Smith. He got up from his seat beside Virginia, which left
Aloysius free to attend to the fast scorching dinner, and broke in on
Maude and Una. They were inclined to quarrel on and ignore him, but
he eventually forced them to silence and proceeded to tell his story in
as few words as possible.

To his surprise, they showed no anger at all, but they gave him a
flattering attention. When he had finished, Una asked tensely, "An
elderly man? With a black goatee?"

Jim nodded. "Black hair, tall and thin."

Una turned abruptly and walked out of the wing, and as Jim stared
after her, Maude put a hand on his arm. "It's all right, Jim. She's a little
upset, naturally. And of course you're right. We'll have to report it to
the police at once."

She hurried out of the wing, closing the door behind her, and
found Una sitting on the burgundy-colored carpeting of the stairs, her
soft gray chiffon spread out around her.

Her face looked peaceful and happy.

"Oh, Maude," she said softly, "it was Father, all right, no doubt about
it. Now I don't have to marry Bert or go back to Ed, or even—"

"Or even bother with Wister any more," Maude finished angrily.

Una colored into the roots of her dark, shining hair and raised frightened gray eyes to Maude's face, and at the same time Wister suddenly emerged from behind, the stairs.

"Oh, yes she does," he said quietly. "Una and I are going to be married."

CHAPTER 19

MAUDE HAD ABSORBED three cocktails rather rapidly, and although she was not drunk, they had made her oblivious to the ridiculous. She squared her shoulders and took on Oliver's P's role.

She ordered Una upstairs and told her, gravely, that she would deal with her later. Una gathered up her chiffon and mounted the stairs with her head held high and a dark color burning in her cheeks. She was vastly uncomfortable, but also vastly relieved to be able to run away and leave everything to Maude.

"Now," Maude said, looking Wister in the, eye, "what do you mean by this absurd nonsense? If my sister has foolishly given you any encouragement, I apologize for her, but you should have had more sense than to take it seriously. You must surely realize that a marriage is utterly out of the question."

She was rather pleased with that, and gave a fleeting thought to the fact that Oliver P. could not have done it better.

But Wister held her eye without flinching and replied firmly, "This is a democratic country, and the person with the most money is the person in the highest station. Therefore, since I now have a good deal more money than Miss—than Una, a marriage would be perfectly justified. It would raise her to her former station in life."

Maude was floored. When she was able to speak, she asked almost feebly, "What do you mean by saying you have plenty of money?"

"Just what I say. I have always been a saving man, and lately I have been very successful with my investments."

"But you—you couldn't have that much."

"Yes," said Wister with a great deal of dignity, "I have. In the old days, when your father was alive and flourishing, a man in my position was able to make a considerable sum over and above his basic salary.

Commissions, tips, and things of that sort. I have saved it, I have invested it, and I have plenty."

Maude was impressed. "Well, that may be," she said mildly, "but it would hardly be fitting for my sister to marry her own butler." She added, after a moment, and with a faint gleam in her eye, "Unless you went away and came back again with a mustache and a new name."

Wister moved his hand in an impatient gesture. "I am not ashamed of my name, or my bare face. But naturally we shall go away after our marriage."

"You know that Una is engaged to Dr. Hanson?"

Wister allowed himself a faint and unmistakably supercilious smile. "Una is impulsive and warmhearted. She made the engagement in order to set me free on a mistaken conviction that she is not the right wife for me. It must be broken tonight, while you are at dinner. I have told her so."

He removed a watch from his waistcoat and raised his eyebrows at it. "It is time for you to go or you will be late." He started to bow but stopped himself and instead said, "*Au revoir*," and made off to his newly discarded kitchen. Maude found that her mouth was sagging open. She closed it with a snap and began to mount the stairs, her hand itching to box Una's ears.

Una was artistically arranged on a chaise longue in her bedroom, pretending to read a book, and Maude stalked over, pulled it out of her hands, and threw it onto the floor.

"Why don't you behave yourself?" she demanded heatedly.

Una raised her arms above her head and said, "Oh, shut up."

"My God! You ought to be put away somewhere. That fool down there has his life all planned, and yours too, and boasting like a gentleman that he has wagonloads of money."

Una nodded her smooth, dark head and giggled. "He has, too."

"He says you're going to give Bert the gate tonight and marry him."

"I'm going to get rid of Bert, yes," Una admitted, "but not for Wister's sake. And as for Ed, he can go and drown himself in whiskey and pink garters. I'm going to do some traveling. Look, Maude, we might as well sell the house. After all, we'll never get a higher price for it than right now. We can split what we get and then I'm going away.

In fact, I want to go away right now. I don't like it around here any more."

"I know you don't," Maude said grimly, "because you've got yourself into such a tangle that even Houdini couldn't unravel you."

Una shivered and for a moment her face pinched up with the old fear.

"Oh, for God's sake!" Maude exclaimed irritably. "Don't start being scared again. It makes my spine crawl when you get that look on you."

She tapped at her lip with her forefinger for a moment and then said suddenly, "Pack your things and get out tonight, if you like. I'll tell Bert, I'll tell Wister, and I'll tell Ed. As long as you've already departed, they'll have nothing to say that will matter, particularly."

Una's face opened out like a flower and her eyes sparkled with eagerness.

"Oh, Maude, that would be wonderful! Simply heavenly! To get right away tonight and save all the unpleasantness and the silly scenes—"

"Save you, yes, but I'll have to see them through," Maude observed dryly.

Una never even heard her. "I'll just pack an overnight case and go straight to New York. I can stay with Bea until you're able to send me some money. Only don't tell anyone where I am, will you?"

Maude nodded. "I'll keep it under my hat. You can catch the nine-fifteen. And for heaven's sake, if you're going to make a new life for yourself, try and behave with a bit more decency."

"Oh, I shall! Una cried gaily. "I'll be a lamb—I promise." She kissed Maude and added happily, "Good-by, darling. You sell the house, then come and join me and we'll have some fun."

Maude left, and Una began to make her preparations. She glanced out of the window from time to time and eventually saw Wister leave. She made a little face and said under her breath, "That gets rid of him."

But she hated to be alone in that great, silent house. It had always depressed her and she began to hurry. Her fingers seemed all thumbs but she eventually got some necessities together, and then she could not find her suitcase. She searched rather frantically for some time before she remembered that she and Maude had piled all the suitcases in a large closet in the right wing. She swore softly, because the closet was in the room that they always called the museum and she hated that room. She hated the suit of armor that looked as though it were alive, she hated the fantastic painting on the walls, but most of all she hated the three antique coffins of different types that Oliver P. had bought and cherished among his most prized possessions.

She stood in the center of her room, frowning into space and asking herself how she could possibly take her things into New York in a brown paper bag. It would look so odd, and what would Bea think? No, better make an effort and go down to the museum for her own bag. It was a beautiful little thing of navy-blue leather with real tortoiseshell fittings that were capped and trimmed with gold.

She went out into the hall and walked resolutely down the stairs. It was beginning to get dark and the lower hall was shadowy until she hurried over and switched on the light. She went to the right wing, where the key was in the lock, as usual, and she turned it and opened the door. She had an odd moment of wishing that the key had not been there, so that she could not have entered the wing, but shook it away as an absurdity.

Just inside the door, she hesitated, peering nervously into the shadows of the huge musty room. As a child, she had always been afraid of the great crystal chandelier in the museum, of the way it suddenly flooded light down onto all the frightening things that were grouped beneath it. Everything would be very still and quiet, but the child Una had always had an impression that just before the light poured over everything, all the horrid curiosities had been engaged in some dark and evil occupation of their own.

She shuddered, and to rid her mind of that old, childish panic, she reached out and pressed the electric switch. There was a click but no answering flood of light, and Una whispered shakily, "Oh damn!"

She remembered then that they had once left the light burning in here for three weeks, each accusing the other of having forgotten to turn it off, and after that they had thrown the main switch in the basement. There were three main switches, one for each wing and one for the main part of the house.

She set her teeth and decided that she was not going all the way down to the cellar just to get some light. She'd walk straight across to that closet and grope. If she could not find her own suitcase, she'd take another. She started into the darkness and made herself walk, although she wanted to run. She had broken out in a cold sweat and was shivering. When she passed the suit of armor she tried to keep her mind a blank and yet was quite conscious of the fact that she half expected it to raise an arm and tap her on the shoulder.

By the time she reached the closet, she was quite ready to snatch at any suitcase and run. She opened the door, and her groping hand almost immediately closed over a leather handle. She pulled and met with resistance, and then began to pull, wildly, and frantically, until something toppled over and crashed down onto her foot. For a moment she was lost to everything but pain, and then she stooped over, sweating and almost crying, to pick up whatever had fallen.

It felt very much like her own little case, so that she clung to it with her left hand and backed out of the closet, feeling with her right hand for the knob of the door so that she could close it.

But instead of the knob she touched a cool, clammy, human hand.

CHAPTER 20

MAUDE PUT IN A VERY uninteresting evening with Bert. She told him about Una's defection before she was well inside the door and he froze immediately. She could not blame him for that, of course, but she had a definite impression that he was as much annoyed about the waste of the food that Una was not there to eat as he was about being cast off. He remarked, at least three times, that he hated to see good food spoiling when people all over the world had not enough,

He left her to prepare cocktails with his own hands, and when he returned with two glasses on a tray Maude dutifully sipped, although she privately decided that it tasted like medicated lemonade. Morbid curiosity prompted her to ask for the recipe, and Bert handed it to her, already carefully written out and, apparently in anticipation of such a request, from his waistcoat pocket. Maude folded the little slip of paper and placed it in her old but once beautiful needlepoint purse, reflecting that she'd save it for Ed. Ed always had enjoyed a good joke.

During the course of dinner and through the grim hours that followed, Bert discussed economic conditions. He and Maude held decidedly different views, but tonight she listened quietly and even nodded once or twice because she felt sorry for him. But it seemed to be wasted effort, since he became just as furious as when she argued with him. Although she had not mentioned her views on this occasion, he kept insisting that her ideas were narrow and bigoted and would certainly drag the country down to disaster.

At eleven he yawned widely and Maude stood up at once.

"Very pleasant evening, Bert," she lied glibly, "but you need sleep and I'm going now so that you can get it. You really work too hard."

This usually pleased him but tonight he merely looked glumly at her and murmured something, with an utter lack of conviction, about the evening being still young.

He accompanied her to her door and left with a brief "Good night." Maude watched him as he made his way back across the street and sighed impatiently for Una's misbehavior. There was something utterly ruthless about Una, she thought uncomfortably. She did not care how many people were hurt when she reached out for what she wanted.

The door to the left wing was partly open and the sound of voices came drifting through. Maude looked up and then headed in that direction like a homing pigeon.

They were all sitting around the living room, including Ed and a man who was strange to Maude. She sank into a seat and said to Ed, "A drink, quickly."

"Sure thing." Ed sprang to his feet and began to rattle glasses and ice. "Where's Una?"

Maude sat back with a relaxing feeling that this would be easy. "She's gone for good. She's not marrying Bert, or you, or, er—" She stopped on the verge of saying, "or Wister," and giggled helplessly.

"Hell's sake," Ed said, staring, at her. "Where did she go? I'll follow her up."

"Do you really want her back?" Maude asked idly.

Ed handed her a drink and said heartily, "Sure thing."

The stranger cleared his throat and murmured, "I don't believe I've had the pleasure."

Maude gave him a sour look and Ed swung around.

"Oh yeah. Maudie, this is a friend of mine, Alex Viter. He's an amateur detective. He untangles knots like crazy and he's much better than the police. I asked him to come and figure out this problem here—"

"I still think we ought to go to the police," Jim interposed.

Aloysius, who had been busy at the bar, came back with a glass in his hand and asked, "You mean Una isn't going to marry Bert after all?"

"Well—" Maude began, and was firmly drowned out by Viter.

"I'm afraid we're wasting time. I haven't all the details of this problem yet and the sooner I start, the sooner it will be cleared up."

Maude gave him an uneasy glance. If he unearthed the fact that Father and P.X. Smith were the same, there would be trouble all around. She tried to look casually at her fingernails but gave it up as the polish was in its usual state of half on and half off. When she looked up again, she found Viter staring at her, so that she drank the rest of her highball too quickly and took to smoothing her hair back.

She need not have worried, for Viter was only admiring her. His wife had died two years before and lately he had been looking for a new one, although he would not have admitted this to anyone, much less himself.

Jim moved over beside him and gave him the entire story of P.X. Smith in detail. Viter removed his mind from Maude and put it on the problem, since he believed in one thing at a time

When Jim had finished, Viter leaned back and studied the ceiling. "Of course the most obvious explanation is that Smith surprised a thief in the living, room and was killed. The intruder perhaps figured that the best way to stop an investigation was to hide the body and did so."

"Well, that sounds reasonable," Aloysius conceded. "All we have to do is find the body."

Viter gave a judicial nod. Virginia spoke for the first time.

"You seem to be leaving out the goatee. Why would any ordinary thief cut it off and bury it in the tomato bed, while he hid the body somewhere else?"

Viter gave her his full attention for a moment, decided that she was too young for him, and then considered her remark. After a moment he said, "Possibly it was intended to change the appearance of the victim so that identification would be difficult."

Virginia looked at her own carefully polished nails and was not convinced.

Viter saw that she wasn't and since he was not convinced himself, he decided to stop theorizing and start a search of the house. He voiced this intention and was loudly overruled by the majority. They all wanted to sleep and had no intention of being awakened by Viter peering under their beds. He was told to postpone his search until the morning. There was some discussion as to where he was to sleep, and after he had refused to bunk in with Ed, he was given a dusty, long-unused room in the main house. Maude cursed quietly as she went to look for sheets, then cursed again when she could find only one. She wavered between using one of the sheets from Una's bed and a very fine old white embroidered spread. She decided on the spread, at last, and used it for a top sheet, hoping, without too much concern, that the embroidery would not scratch him. She used Una's pillowcase to dust off the tops of the furniture and then wondered, without caring, whether it would ever be clean again.

She was tired of the whole thing by this time and determined to tell Aloysius that if he had any more guests, he'd have to bed them down in his own part of the house. Which brought her to the realization that she had decided to let them all stay on. There was no longer any reason for turning them out. She made up her mind to charge Aloysius a hundred a month. It would be a nice addition to her new and improved income.

She had had several uneasy moments when she wondered whether there could possibly be any mistake about P.X. Smith having been Father, but she put them firmly away, only to face a guilty realization that she and Una were merely relieved and happy about their father's death. But it was no use, she thought, trying to work up any grief. He had never meant much to them. He hadn't noticed them except to scold or correct. The truth was that they had not even seen very much of him.

Viter came to the door as she finished smoothing the bed and said playfully, "A penny for your thoughts."

"Only a short time ago," said Maude obscurely, "I'd have sold, even for a penny. Good night. I hope you'll be comfortable."

He bowed and wished her good night, and she brushed past him and headed for her own room. She passed Una's on the way and went in to smooth the spread over the now naked pillow. She had turned to go when her eye fell on a chair near the dressing table and she stopped short, while a chill prickled along her spine and over her scalp.

The chair supported a little pile of exquisite underwear, a satin-finished, rubberized toilet bag, and a bottle of Una's vitamin pills.

Why, she hasn't gone, after all, Maude thought wildly.

CHAPTER 21

MAUDE STOOD AND TRIED to gather her confused thoughts into some sort of order. Una had always been a scatterbrained packer on the few occasions when she had been forced to do it for herself. Her usual procedure was to inveigle someone into doing it for her. Perhaps, Maude thought, she had gathered this stuff together and then decided to buy everything new and so had left it.

She went to the chair and turned over the underwear. It was Una's best. There was also a silk blouse that she wore only with her most expensive suit. With all the money in the world, she would not be able to buy underwear and a blouse like that these days. And in any case, why would she leave the vitamin pills? She was always saying that they were absolutely indispensable to her.

Maude paced the room once or twice and then veered over to the closet and looked through it. Well, Una's precious little suitcase was gone, anyway. Perhaps she had been stocking up on new underwear without telling anyone, possibly with money she had picked up from Wister. But even that did not explain the vitamin pills. And why would she bring out the old underwear and pile it on a chair?

Maude suddenly stopped her restless pacing and snapped her fingers. They had put all the suitcases into that closet in the right wing.

She'd go down at once and see whether any was missing. Una's favorite little navy-blue fitted case should be gone. Surely it would be.

She went downstairs, telling herself all the way that the case would not be there and that there was no doubt a reasonable explanation for everything. She went through the hall and into the right wing, where she switched on the light. The great crystal chandelier no longer contained its full complement of bulbs, so that it gave out only a pale white light that washed over the museum with almost the effect of moonlight.

Maude shivered. It was a grim place to come to at night, she thought, or any other time, for that matter. She wished that she had brought Ed along, although he never had been much good in the role of male protector. If anything scared him, he'd run like the wind.

Maude took a long breath and walked firmly and quickly across to the closet. The light was bad in that corner but it did not matter, because Una's suitcase was the first thing that met her eye. It was standing by itself just inside the door, separate from the pile of luggage directly behind it. Maude looked at it for a moment and then gave way to a panic that had been slowly accumulating. She picked up the case and fled from the wing.

She had reached the front hall of the main house before she thought at all. The first thing that slid into her mind was the fact that she had left the light on in the museum. It made her shudder to think of that great room, empty and still, fixed in that pale, chilly light from the chandelier. She'd have to go back and turn it off. There was no help for it. She'd never be able to sleep for thinking of all those grim relics frozen in eerie white light.

She straightened her back, called herself a fool, and walked back to the wing. As she approached the door, she thought she heard some sort of a noise, but she told herself again not to be a fool and pushed in without any hesitation. The light was off.

She stood for a moment, frightened, and wondering confusedly whether she had made a mistake, and then she forced herself to stretch an arm and press the switch.

The ghastly room lit up as usual, but she barely glanced at it before she turned the light off again and fled.

But as she went up the stairs she was bothered by an impression of something wrong. There had been some disarrangement in the museum and her conscience told her that she should go back and find out what it was. Her body, however, paid no heed to this command. It went straight up to her bedroom, still clutching Una's little suitcase.

In the familiarity and comfort of her own room, she began to relax, and decided not to worry her head about any disarrangement in the museum. She hated the place and wouldn't care if she never saw it again.

She examined the suitcase, admiring it even as she worried about Una. It was a beautiful little thing and certainly you could not buy anything to compare with it today. Even if Una had decided to take nothing with her to Bea's, she'd have taken the suitcase anyway. She had been longing to use it for some time past.

Maude felt helpless and thoroughly frightened. She would have decided, comfortably, that there was some simple explanation had it not been for the affair of P.X. Smith.

She felt that she had to do something, and wondered whether she ought to call the police. Only, she'd look silly if Una turned up at Bea's, after all. Well, that was it, of course. She must phone Bea at once. She went out into the hall where there was an upstairs telephone.

Viter was slowly pacing his bedroom with a look of inward satisfaction. A puzzle of this sort was the kind of thing he liked. A touch of the ridiculous, as supplied by the goatee, with the dark background of a possible murder. In fact, the murder was probable. The goatee gave substance to Aloysius's story, so that apparently the old man had been murdered, his goatee cut off and hidden in the garden while his body was hidden somewhere else. Viter considered for a moment and then shook his head. No, the tomato bed had already been disturbed when Virginia found the goatee there, so that the body had probably been buried there originally. Then the murderer had thought of a better hiding place and had removed the body and forgotten the goatee.

Viter rubbed his hands together and decided that he was progressing. He took another turn about the room and then started violently when Maude knocked on the door.

The sight of Maude took his mind off business and put it on the future, and he bowed her into the room with a good deal of manner. She advanced only a step or two and explained, without preamble, that she felt she should contact the police but that she wanted to talk to him first. Actually her reason for coming to him was a faint hope that he could offer a simple explanation for Una's disappearance, something that she had been too tired and confused to think of. She did not tell him about Una's tangled love affairs. He was to unearth that for himself, later.

He could not explain Una's absence but he took the problem in hand with confidence. "The first thing, Mrs. Watson, is to search the entire house. You have ascertained, by telephone, that your sister did not arrive at her friend's home in New York. Now, there are two possibilities: something happened en route or she is still here. A person could always slip and fall, you know, and lie unconscious in some obscure corner. We must check on that before we do anything else."

"It will take some time," Maude said, trying to keep her voice steady. "It's a large house. We'll go to the main attic first, I think. She might have gone up there for something."

Viter followed her, feeling pleased. He had wanted to search earlier on, but they had overruled him and told him to go to bed. Now he had a chance of unraveling the whole thing before morning.

Ed, lying on his back in bed and staring at the ceiling, heard them go with a sigh of relief. He was a fussy sleeper and Viter had kept him awake, pacing back and forth. But now he had gone off somewhere with Maude and everything was quiet. Ed liked Maude. She was a good sort and he didn't mind what she did. It never occurred to him to put an innocent construction upon what he had heard. He merely put Maude down as a fast worker. Or perhaps it was Viter who was the fast worker. Ed yawned and turned over to go to sleep.

The next minute he was up on his elbow, swearing at the tenants in the left wing. One of them was walking slowly up the uncarpeted stairs and Ed could hear each footfall quite distinctly. And then, when the person must have been about halfway up, the footsteps ceased entirely. Ed strained his ears until the sweat started out on his forehead but the footsteps did not continue up, nor did they go down again.

CHAPTER 22

VIRGINIA WAS THE LAST to use the bathroom that night. She had washed some underwear and taken a long, soaking bath. When at last she emerged into the darkened hall she felt soothed and relaxed.

Jim was waiting for her just outside his door and he said in a low voice, "I have an outsize headache. Would you be kind enough to come into my room and massage my forehead?"

Virginia frowned at him. "Don't be ridiculous. Just take a couple of aspirins."

"I have and it hasn't helped a bit. I need someone to massage my head and then I think I can get off to sleep."

"That's just plain nonsense."

"My head," said Jim in a dignified voice, "is peculiar."

"Yes, of course. We all know that but it's nothing that can be helped by massage. It needs a surgical operation to remove the present brain and substitute some plush, which will probably work better."

"Very funny," said Jim gravely. "Will you do me this trifling kindness or shall I be obliged to wake Susan, who is sound asleep and probably dreaming of Gus?"

"Oh, for God's sake!" Virginia muttered. "I'll knead your blasted head for a minute or two and then I'm going to bed, ready or not."

Jim grinned at her and stood aside as she entered his room. He placed a comfortable chair beside the bed, seated her in it, and then stretched himself out with a sigh of satisfaction.

She gave him a suspicious look and began to knead his forehead vigorously. He stood it for a while and then said mildly, "Not quite so much enthusiasm."

Virginia relaxed the pressure, more because she was getting tired than for any other reason, and he murmured, "Ah, that's nice. That ought to fix me up."

"I can't understand a doctor stooping to old-fashioned methods of this sort," Virginia said crossly.

Jim closed his eyes. "My grandmother used to swear by it and what's good enough for her is good enough for me.

"You know, I like this left wing. If Maude would only be reasonable,

I'd like to rent it and have my office here."

"You'd have competition with Dr. Hanson right across the street."

"Let him attend to his pills and I'll attend to mine," Jim said comfortably. "Anyway, with the two of us practicing within spitting distance and not another doctor in town, it would make a sort of medical center."

"If you bought the whole house, eventually, you'd be doing better than Hanson, wouldn't you?"

"That's my ambition. The Graham mansion. The tattered, barefoot Larson boy grown up to inhabit the biggest house in town."

"That's hardly fair to your parents," Virginia said severely. "You were neatly dressed, at least when you left your house in the morning, and you always wore shoes."

Jim did not seem to be listening. He added dreamily, "And married to one of the Graham girls."

"Aren't they a bit old for you?" Virginia asked.

"Old?" He looked at her. "Oh, I don't mean Maude or Una, I mean you. You're a Graham."

"So I am but well out of *your* reach."

"I have a long arm when I stretch for something I want. If I were to save your old man from a fate worse than death, or something, I think he'd come over to my side. And perhaps you would too."

"I can always keep Father out of trouble by tying him to a post in the back yard while I'm at work," Virginia said, yawning. "So don't think you can work anything along those lines."

Jim grinned up at the ceiling. "Aloysius knew his way around when he was no more than three years old, I should judge, but you seem to have a very naive and touching faith in him. Keep it. Such childish innocence is becoming to a sweet young girl."

"You're jealous of Father," Virginia said serenely, "because he knows how to have fun and you don't. Listen, how can you jabber away like this when you have such a frightful headache?"

"The pain seems to drain away as soon as your soft hands touch my forehead. You've no idea—"

Virginia stood up. "I don't want to have any idea. I'm going to bed."

She started for the door but at the same time a sliver of light appeared under the door that connected with Aloysius's room, and the next instant his voice arose in such a cascade of lurid language that Virginia stopped and Jim raised his head from the pillow so that he could hear better. They both listened for some time before they gathered that the temperamental bedside lamp in Aloysius's room had suddenly lit up and awakened him from a sound sleep.

Virginia made a vexed sound with her tongue and walked out of Jim's room just as Aloysius slammed out of his. The sight of his daughter emerging from the hated Larson's room in her dressing gown drove the breath from Aloysius's body, so that Virginia had time to pass the remark that he was always getting excited about nothing.

Aloysius recovered his breath and poured a full-bodied flood of invective and abuse over her blonde head.

Ed, who had come to investigate the stairs and the footsteps which had stopped halfway up and had found nothing, was diverted by Aloysius's eloquence and stood still in admiring silence. Jim had appeared at his door and when Aloysius stopped, of necessity, for breath, he said bravely, "I'll marry her if you insist, sir."

Both Aloysius and Virginia turned on him and yelled, "Shut up!" And then Virginia turned on her father and had her say. She informed him, without mincing any words, that his mind was so filthy that it dwelt in the gutter. She told him several more things, as they occurred to her, and Aloysius fell silent, while a dark flush spread over his face.

When Virginia had finished at last, Ed said softly, "Atta girl."

Aloysius gave Ed an evil side glance and changed his tactics. "But what *were* you doing in the louse's bedroom, honey?" he asked almost gently.

"I was answering a call for help," Virginia snapped, "and I always shall answer a call for help. I don't care what kind of a louse it comes from."

"There's nothing special about me," Jim interposed. "I'm just an ordinary louse."

"But look at him, honey," Aloysius whined. "He appears to be in the pink of health. Why would he be needing help?"

"Well," Ed said, trying to keep the peace, "seems to me he looks a bit pale."

Aloysius didn't think so, but decided to let the whole thing drop.

He turned to Ed and asked belligerently, "What the hell are you doing here?"

Ed explained the mysterious footsteps in great detail and finished up by saying, "I couldn't stand it. I had to come and see. As far as I'm concerned, that person stopped halfway up the stairs and should be there yet, but he isn't."

"You mean you can hear what goes on in this wing from the main part of the house?" Aloysius demanded, thinking of a remark or two he had made about Maude when she was safely out of the wing.

Ed shook his head. "No, it isn't that. It's just that my room seems to be a sounding board for these stairs. I can always hear the slightest noise on them. Some sort of architectural mistake, maybe. I don't know."

"Perhaps there's a secret panel halfway up the stairs," Aloysius suggested, finding himself rather intrigued with the idea.

"No extra space there," Ed said. "I've been looking it over. Must be some other explanation."

Aloysius lost interest and went back to his original trouble. "I wish," he said peevishly, "that someone would discover a reason for my light going on and off by itself. I can't get it to go on when I want to read by it but it always lights up just after I've gone to sleep."

"Let me have a look at it," Jim said, walking into Aloysius's room with an air of authority. Aloysius and Ed followed, while Virginia came as far as the door.

Jim first unscrewed the bulb, which threw the room into darkness, except for a faint glow from the downstairs hall light. He then screwed it in again, and the light came on. "The bulb is all right," he announced gravely. "There may be a defective switch, perhaps." He walked out into the hall and scratched his head.

"Brilliant!" Aloysius sneered. "We are all speechless with admiration!"

"You won't be speechless," said Jim, "when they bury you."

He walked toward the stairs and stopped at the head. "You say it never goes on when you first get into bed and want to read?"

"Never," said Aloysius sourly.

"But it always goes on sometime during the night?"

"Always."

"Then you switch it off and it goes off?"

"Yes."

Jim thought for a moment and then asked absently, "Have you any flatulence or belching after meals?"

Aloysius glared at him, and he added hastily, "No, no, I mean, at night you go and switch the lamp on, and it won't go on?"

"Yes."

"And you leave it switched on, although it hasn't lit up?"

"I guess so," Aloysius said impatiently.

Jim nodded. "When you first go to bed everybody is up here going to bed too. Some of them have lights on in their rooms but the hall light is off, and I think that's what it is. I knew of a case like that once before."

"What do you mean?" Ed asked curiously, and Aloysius muttered, "Drivel, as usual."

Jim smoothed his hair back with the flat of his hand. "You boys wait up here and tell me whether the light goes off."

He went down the stairs and switched off the hall light. Ed and Aloysius shouted that the lamp had gone off too. Jim switched the hall light on again, and the male chorus announced that the lamp was also on.

Jim came back up the stairs. "Mr. Graham," he said formally, "it is merely a matter of defective wiring. The line from your lamp is tapped onto a wrong line. I could explain it to you but it would be difficult, and perhaps impossible, for you to follow me. Actually it means that if you want your lamp on, the hall light must be on as well."

Aloysius muttered, "I see," and tried wildly to think of some insulting remark, without success.

Virginia, who had been silent for some time, said slowly, "Then someone is coming in every night, someone we don't know about, who is turning on the hall light down there."

CHAPTER 23

"ONE THINGS SEEMS fairly clear," Jim observed, rumpling his hair. "Whoever has been turning that light on also met up with P.X. Smith."

Virginia nodded. "He didn't know that anyone was here or he would not have gone around turning lights on."

"Depends on what he was doing here," Jim said. "In fact, what was he doing here?"

"We know one thing he did here, to P.X. Smith," Aloysius remarked callously.

"Smith was killed simply because he was in the way," Jim said, and added, "If he *was* killed."

"Listen!" Aloysius shouted, and Ed broke in, "That's wacky. Who'd kill a guy just because he was there?"

"My light went off and on before P.X. showed up," Aloysius said, diverted. "And who knew P.X. was coming here, anyway? So it certainly looks like they croaked him because they stubbed a toe on him. Maybe they'd come back and clean up the rest of us if they knew we were here."

Ed doubled his fists and muttered, "Not if I see him first."

Virginia glanced at him. "You're all right. You're not living in this wing."

Ed said, "Yeah, that's right," with a long breath of relief, and his hands relaxed.

"I still think it's a case for the police," Jim said stubbornly.

"No, no," Ed protested. "Viter can handle it. Give the guy a chance."

"Well, suppose we go and tell him about this light business. That's one thing he doesn't know about."

"Godssake! You sent the guy to bed and wouldn't let him search, and now you want to go and yank him out of bed to tell him about lights."

"Oh, nonsense!" Virginia said impatiently. "What investigator who was worth his salt would sleep the night away? He'll want to hear about the lights."

"Yes, well, but he's human too," Ed murmured feebly.

Aloysius, who felt secure because Virginia was on his side, said stoutly, "He's no more human than we are, not so much. Does he think he can snore on his fat back while we creep around here in fear of our lives? Don't forget that light went on tonight. Maybe the murdering fella is right in here with us now."

"Nah," Ed said, "that was me. I turned the light on and then came up to hear you swearing like a trooper."

"Oh," Aloysius considered for a moment and then said excitedly, "But you heard those footsteps go up the stairs and stop halfway. That's why you came in here."

"He probably was dreaming,'" Jim said. "I'm going to yank Viter out of bed and see if I can get a little action. If he won't do anything, I'm calling in the police at once."

He strode off with a determined look on his face and Aloysius and Ed followed. Virginia hesitated but trailed after them in the end, because she didn't like the idea of being left alone. Nobody gave a thought to Susan, who was sleeping peacefully and presumably still dreaming of Gus.

As it happened, she woke up shortly after they had all gone and was unable to get back to sleep. She could see, through the darkness, that Virginia was not in her bed, and supposed, with only a faint uneasiness, that she was still in the bathroom.

The wing was absolutely still and silent and Susan presently fumbled on the bedside table for a cigarette. She puffed nervously, waiting for Virginia to come back, trying to fight a growing sense of fear. It was unusual for her to wake again after she had once gone to sleep, and she supposed it was because of all the queer things that had been happening. She was nervous—anyone would be nervous—and anyhow where was Virginia? Why was she taking so long in that flossy bathroom? It would be awful to have to sleep alone, especially when you were a bit nervous, what with the ghost of Oliver P. roaming through the wing.

Susan choked on a mouthful of smoke and glanced uneasily in the direction of the door. Where *was* Virginia? Had she drowned in the tub or something? She tried to look at her wristwatch by the light of her cigarette but it was a failure. The wristwatch was a streamlined number with slim hands which were ever coy about indicating the exact time. She strained her ears to hear some sound from the bathroom but there was not even the dripping of a tap. Her cigarette had burned down to a stub and she fumbled for the ashtray and put it out. She was too stimulated now to lie still and she presently slipped out of bed and went to the door. She peered out and saw a faint glow from the downstairs hall light and another, brighter light from behind Aloysius's half-opened door. The bathroom door stood wide open, revealing a dark and seemingly empty space.

Susan tried to quell her growing panic by telling herself that Virginia was in her father's room. She *must* be in her father's room. And yet there should be the sound of their voices but everything was so still. She walked quickly to Aloysius's room and knocked on the door. There was no answer and no sound, and she went in and gave a frightened glance around. The bedside lamp glowed eerily in the empty room.

Susan caught her breath, backed out, and ran into Jim's room, her only thought now being a frantic desire for human company. There was no electric light in Jim's room but it was brilliant with moonlight and she could see that the bed was empty. As she stood there, with her breath coming short, fighting panic, she became conscious of a regular tapping against the windowpane.

It was Oliver P., Susan thought hysterically. He was driving them all out. He had driven all the others away and now he was warning her to go. She stood perfectly still, too frightened to move or even to scream. Then she heard a noise in the attic.

They are all up there, she thought wildly, and felt that she must get to them at once. Her legs were cold and numb but she managed to back out of the room and began a terrified scramble up the attic stairs. Her first momentum slowed, as the darkness closed around her, and the sound she had heard faded out into silence. It was suddenly as still in the attic as it had been downstairs. She stopped beside a small window at the head of the stairs and as she stood there, the utter stillness was broken by a sharp tapping on the outside of the pane.

Susan thought that she screamed and then realized that no sound had come from her paralyzed throat. The low, hoarse scream that she heard had come from someone else. Her legs gave way and she sagged against the banister. Almost drowsily, she thought of Oliver P. again. He was right beside her now, his heavy breathing was in her ears as she drifted away into oblivion.

CHAPTER 24

VIRGINIA HEARD THE scream from a small sewing room at the back part of the main house where she was helping in the search for Una, under Viter's direction. They had found him and Maude in the attic and he had taken charge of them as though they were a troop of children. They were all assigned to various areas of the vast house and cautioned to look inside closets and under beds.

Virginia was obliged to admit to herself that she was distinctly nervous. She did not like being alone in that huge house with only a few scattered people. The scream, when she heard it, seemed muted and far away, and she thought it had come from the attic above her. She went up at once, only to find Viter busily moving some old, discarded furniture.

He listened to her attentively and then made a hasty search of the attic without finding anything. He pondered for a moment before deciding that the sound must have come from one of the attics in the right and left wings. They were on a lower level than the main attic, and there was no connection, so he was obliged to go all the way down to the ground floor, while Virginia flew after him, trying not to trip on the hem of her robe.

Aloysius was seated on the bottom step of the stairs and he cocked an alert eye at them.

"You finished?"

"No," said Viter. "Have you?"

"Yep. Can't find a sign of her. My idea is that she's hiding out on us. She always was a pest and old Oliver P. made her worse because he had no more idea of how to bring up girls than a monkey."

"Come with me," Viter said, hurrying toward the right wing.

"Wait a minute," Virginia called. "If that scream came from one of the wings, I'm pretty sure it was the left wing."

Viter changed his course without stopping and made for the left wing. Virginia and Aloysius followed close behind but took care not to get ahead of him.

The left wing was in darkness, and Viter began to grope for the light switch in the hall. Aloysius, more familiar with its location, found it for him and remarked uneasily, "We left this light on, I know we did."

Viter nodded without comment and started up the stairs to investigate the scream. It had to be investigated, he knew, although he felt that it was quite possibly a figment of a girl's overexcited imagination.

The attic was in darkness and Viter pulled out his pocket flashlight and played it around. Susan's limp body was highlighted almost immediately in its white glow. Viter thought that they had found Una until Virginia cried in horror, "It's Susan! She's been hurt!"

Susan opened her eyes and began feebly to pull herself up by the banister, until Viter and Virginia raised her between them. They helped her down the stairs. Aloysius followed, shouting questions at Susan as to what had happened and directions at her supporters about getting her downstairs and into her own room.

They got her into bed among them, after having replaced the smashed electric bulb with one from Jim's room, and were about to feed her aspirins when Jim appeared and told them to stop manhandling her and leave her to him. He went to his room to get something for her. They could hear him muttering peevishly as he stumbled around in the dark. There was no reply to his anguished question as to who had stolen his bulb. Susan clutched at Virginia's hands and said with chattering teeth, "Don't ever leave me like that again, not in this awful place. Phone Gus."

"What for?" Virginia asked. "You're not engaged to him, are you?"

"No," said Susan, still chattering, "but I think I shall be soon."

"Then we won't phone him," Virginia decided firmly. "We're all here with you now and you'll be all right. But tell me what happened. What made you scream?"

"I didn't scream," Susan whispered. "It was somebody—something else."

Viter, who had been standing modestly in the background, advanced to the bed and asked, "Someone else?"

Susan pushed her disordered brown curls back from her forehead and muttered confusedly, "Not somebody—something. It tapped at the windows and screamed and breathed in my ear and I couldn't see. It must have been their father, you know, Oliver P. Graham. He doesn't like to have us living here. This was always his own private place, and he's trying to drive us out."

"Oh, nonsense!" Virginia said, too loudly. "You were frightened, and screamed yourself—you know you did."

"I didn't!" Susan sobbed. "I didn't. It was something right there—"

Jim came back at that point and offended Virginia by saying, "Stop upsetting her." He gave Susan a capsule and a glass of water and said, "Swallow this and go to sleep. Someone will stay in the room with you until you wake up."

Susan swallowed the capsule and whispered, "Are you sure? I won't be alone again. Not in this awful place."

"I'm absolutely sure," Jim said firmly. He watched her for a moment and then walked over to the other side of the room where Viter and Aloysius stood in silence. Virginia joined them and Jim said in a low voice, "I have to go. I've had a call and I'll have to leave at once. But someone will have to stay with Susan. If she wakes up and finds herself alone, she'll be in a bad way."

"I'll stay with her," Virginia said promptly. "But how could you have had a call, when no one knows you're here?"

"My pal who sleeps in the office," Jim explained, turning away. "I told you before. He's fit to be tied, too. Says he's been here over half an hour throwing pebbles at various windows. Keep an eye on Susan, will you? I'll be back as soon as I can make it."

He hurried away, and Virginia turned to Viter. "You see, that explains one part of what frightened Susan—the tapping on the windows, I mean. It was just Jim's friend trying to wake him up. They'd made an arrangement for him to do it that way if any calls came in."

Viter nodded. Virginia was silent for a moment, frowning down at the toe of her slipper. "I suppose she became hysterical," she said presently, "and screamed so loudly that she scared herself. Thought it was someone else."

"Right," said Aloysius in a satisfied voice.

Viter preferred to do his own deducing and shook his head even before a valid objection slid into his mind.

"How about the downstairs light?" he asked with quiet triumph. "You assured me that that was left on. Certainly I don't think Miss Falks turned it off, so I'm inclined to think that she didn't do her own screaming, either."

Aloysius felt a cold chill uncurl itself along his spine. He had been about to go to bed because he was tired and he felt that everything could be left until the morning. But Viter's words brought a picture of his bedside lamp, eerily turning itself on and off, and he was suddenly unable to face his bedroom alone.

Viter departed, and Virginia, after a look at Susan, removed her dressing gown and slipped into bed.

Aloysius cleared his throat.

"I can't leave you girls alone. I wouldn't be easy in my mind about you. I'm going to bunk in here so that I can protect you."

"Good God!" Virginia exclaimed. "Where?"

Aloysius pulled up an armchair with a matching footstool and stretched himself out. "Don't you worry about me," he said comfortably.

Virginia said she wasn't but he was already drowsy and didn't bother to answer. He congratulated himself on being a hardy soul who could bed down almost anywhere and proved it by falling asleep at once.

Virginia lay flat on her back, wondering how she was going to get to work in the morning. She was desperately tired and yet she felt sure that she would not be able to sleep, and she had already taken an afternoon off.

As she lay there, a picture of P.X. Smith drifted into her mind, and at the same time she thought of Oliver P. Graham. Oliver P. had never worn a goatee and yet the uncanny likeness between the two faces struck her with a cold sense of fear.

CHAPTER 25

BERT, TOSSING IN HIS comfortable bed in the house across the street, was also thinking of P.X. Smith. Even with that black goatee the old man had looked uncannily like Oliver P. Graham. You couldn't miss it. Bert had had quite a shock in the restaurant and he hadn't been able to get the thing out of his mind.

He moved his head restlessly on the pillow and then turned over, his legs feeling for a cooler spot on the bed. If only he could sleep. The night seemed to stretch endlessly before him, dark and still and faintly menacing. He thought of Una, telling himself that she was selfish and always had been. Maude was much nicer of the two but then Una was the more attractive. With all her weakness and selfishness, you couldn't help being drawn to her. He thought of her slim little body and the shining dark hair and the mystery of her smoky gray eyes and gritted his teeth. There was no use in fooling himself. She had been going to marry him for his money and no other reason.

He flung the sheet from his perspiring body, got out of bed, and went into the bathroom. He had always avoided taking drugs but he was going to have something now to make him sleep. After all, he had work to do in the morning and a responsibility to his patients. He had to have some sleep. He selected a capsule, swallowed it, and hoped feverishly that there would be no night calls.

He went back to bed and for a while lay quietly on his side, waiting for the drug to work. But his mind seemed to be more active than ever and at last he reached for the cigarettes on the bedside table and lit one. A cigarette might help to relax him; then perhaps he'd be drowsy and could get to sleep.

As he lay there, smoking, he heard Mr. and Mrs. Anderson come in and was instantly infuriated. It was nearly four o'clock and they had to be up early. How could they expect to get any work done during the day if they were out kicking up their heels all night? They seemed to have a good time together, always going out somewhere, and they played cards for money when they certainly couldn't afford it. He'd have to speak to them in no uncertain terms. They could leave his employment if they didn't like it. They needn't suppose he didn't know that they took naps in the daytime to catch up something they had no earthly right to do. He paid them well, far too much, as a matter of fact, for their daytime hours, and simply because he couldn't be standing over them every minute, they stole some of his hours for sleeping. It was stealing and he intended to tell them so. He'd tell them the first thing in the morning and if they gave him any impertinence, they could go. There were other people ready and waiting to take them on, of course. He knew that. Mrs. Anderson was a wonderful cook while Mr. Anderson had the reputation of being able to make a formal English garden in the middle of a desert.

That was another thing. Bert had caught him once giving a hand to

Maude across the street. What right had Maude to steal the services of a gardener to whose support she contributed not one cent? Bert had spoken to Mr. Anderson about it and the man had nearly left. In fact, he would have left had it not been that Mrs. Anderson liked having the house to herself, with no mistress to annoy her. So they had stayed on that time, but lately Mrs. Anderson had begun to hint that Bert, when he was at home, was worse than any mistress she'd ever known.

He crushed out his cigarette, absentmindedly, since there was nearly half of it left, and it was his usual custom to smoke a cigarette until it singed his mouth. All this stewing about the Andersons had temporarily put P.X. Smith and Una's nasty, underhanded treatment of him out of his mind, but as he lay down, he thought of Smith again, vividly, and behind Smith he could see Una's face, lovely, selfish and mocking.

Bert began to weep. He wasn't well and he knew it. Probably the drug was upsetting him but just the same, he was not well. He had worked too hard during the war years. He had given his health to his country, and nobody appreciated it.

The thought that he had made a supreme sacrifice for his country comforted Bert and relaxed him. The drug began to take effect and the fatigue of past weeks caught up with him. He sank into so deep a sleep that he never heard the sound of stealthy footsteps as they went past his door and into his study at the end of the hall.

The intruder was Wister, who had followed the Andersons in. They had been slightly drunk and had forgotten to lock the back door, a fairly common oversight of theirs when they came in late. They were well aware that Bert liked to have the house locked up at night as though it were a fortress, but they always worked on the theory that what Bert didn't know wouldn't hurt him.

So Wister came in and, because he always moved quietly, was able to roam the house at will without disturbing anyone. He was interested in Bert's private affairs—his accounts, bankbooks, correspondence, and so on. He searched the lower floor first, ending up in the library, a room lined with handsomely bound books which apparently had never been used. There was a desk by the window, a rather too ornate piece of heavy, carved mahogany. Its surface was tidy and polished and bore a blotter, inkstand, calendar, and paper knife all finished in red, gold-tooled leather. It all looked as unused as the books and the drawers were mostly empty.

Wister went upstairs. The long corridor was lined with doors, some closed, including the one leading to Bert's bedroom—Wister knew Bert kept his bedroom locked at night—and one at the far end of the hall. That must be the study, Wister thought, and probably it was locked too. He made his way quietly along the length of the corridor and ran into a piece of luck. The study door was locked but Bert had absentmindedly left the key there. Wister turned it and slipped inside.

He closed the door quietly behind him and locked it on the inside. Now he was safe, he thought with quiet satisfaction. If Bert tried to get in, he'd have to search for the key—and he'd never dream that he'd been absentminded enough to leave it in the lock.

Wister closed the window shades, switched on a small lamp, and laughed quietly as he seated himself at the shabby old desk. The one downstairs was on display for visitors but this was obviously where Bert kept his private papers.

Wister began a methodical inspection. As he went patiently through each paper he felt irritation scratching at his nerves. Every item for which Bert spent money was neatly set down, with its price. Aside from marketing, he did a great deal of his shopping in the five-and-ten, and Wister, blinking over "One dishcloth—10¢" and "Two sherry glasses—20¢" began to realize, despairingly, that it would take him days to go through everything. And he could not find what he was looking for. He wanted, specifically, any sum that had been spent on Una, and so far there was nothing of the sort.

He flung himself away from the desk after a while, swearing quietly, and began to search the room for money. But there were no locked drawers, no strongboxes, no safe and, certainly, no money. Apparently, what money of Bert's was not in the bank he kept close beside him. Probably put it in a money belt and wore it to bed, Wister thought contemptuously.

As a matter of fact, this was an injustice. Bert had no money belt. He had seen one once but they had wanted too much for it so he took frequent trips to the bank to get out five dollars at a time and wrote checks when it was unavoidable. At the moment he had three dollars and forty-seven cents with him, most carelessly reposing on the dresser.

But Wister, in his irritation, was exaggerating by this time and would never have believed it. He was convinced that Bert was hiding substantial sums in the house because, for one thing, if he put it all in the bank, he'd have to pay income tax for the full amount. It seemed probable that a great many of his patients paid him in cash and he could easily hide some of it, so that his recorded income would be lower for tax purposes. As it happened, Wister was wrong about that too. Bert worked feverishly to pare his income tax down to a minimum but he paid it all.

Wister left the study and searched through the empty bedrooms and even up in the attic, but he found no money. He came down at last with his lip curled and a conviction that Bert's cash was buried in the back yard.

In the Graham house across the street, the search for Una was slowing down. Viter had told Maude about Susan, and the two of them were drinking coffee in the kitchen, having entirely forgotten Ed, who had been detailed to go through the museum in the right wing. It had been a difficult assignment and Ed had worked his way faithfully and wearily through the vast, cluttered room. He had given up looking for Una and was merely prying, when he found a stack of hundred-dollar bills in one of the small drawers of a Chinese cabinet.

CHAPTER 26

ED HAD ALWAYS BEEN short of cash and he eyed the stack of hundred-dollar bills wistfully, wondering if he had ever before seen so much money at one time. He presently closed the drawer with care and shook his head at the carelessness of the girls in leaving money around like that. He was puzzled, too, at the stingy way in which the house was being run, when there was all this laid away. The girls had always been such spendthrifts.

He closed the outer doors of the Chinese cabinet and gave a last glance around the museum. He'd finished here now and he might as well report to Viter. He left the wing and returned to the main part of the house, where he wandered around for some time without seeing anyone at all. By the time he tracked down Viter and Maude in the kitchen, he was frankly scared of his own footsteps.

Viter was wearing his party manners in an attempt to fascinate Maude. Ed recognized the symptoms at once, since that sort of thing was right down his alley and he was conscious of a spasm of annoyance that he should have been sweating away in that eerie museum while Viter sat comfortably guzzling coffee and making passes at Maude.

Maude had put her concern for Una into the back of her mind and was enjoying herself. She glanced up at Ed, saw that he was in a bad humor, and called cheerfully, "Come and have some coffee. You look worn out."

Ed lowered himself into a chair and gave Viter a suspicious look. "Did you find Una?"

Viter cleared his throat and said in a voice of authority, "No. She is still missing, unless you found her in your department. You are the last to report."

Ed stirred his coffee and shook his head.

"You were a good deal longer over your assignment than I would have thought," Viter observed with touch of severity.

"Hear him, will you?" Ed mumbled, looking injured. "I had a room the size of a skating rink to do, and loaded to the ceiling with junk!" It was just like the guy, he thought, when you had a beef against him, to turn it around so that he was beefing at you."

"Quite so," Viter said smoothly. "But, of course you were not looking for a needle."

Ed blushed and devoted himself to his coffee in silence. He had looked into all sorts of small drawers and boxes simply out of curiosity and you could trust a guy like Viter to bring it up just when it was most embarrassing.

Maude saw that he was uncomfortable and changed the subject.

"Mr. Viter was telling me that that girl Susan ran into some trouble. She went to the attic and thought there was someone up there with her."

Viter raised his shoulders in the suggestion of a shrug and murmured, "Probably hysteria."

"I don't know about that," Ed said uneasily. "There's something the matter with this house and there's something screwy about the people in it, too."

Maude glared at him. "Are you insinuating that I'm off my onion, Ed Randall?"

"Well, no, not so much you, Maudie, but you must admit that Una's been acting as though she ought to be inside. Getting engaged to that mutt Bert."

Viter was immediately interested and began to question Maude about Una and the mutt Bert. She gave a few reluctant and impatient answers and then declared that she was tired to the point of exhaustion and was going to bed. There would certainly be a telegram from Una in the morning, explaining her whereabouts, because she had no money with her and would have to depend on Maude to send some.

Viter nodded and stood up. "Of course, that seems extremely probable. It was very remiss of me to keep you here, asking questions, when you are so fatigued. You must go to bed and try to get some rest."

Maude nodded with reserve, since she knew that nobody ever kept her anywhere when she didn't want to stay. She put the cream and butter into the refrigerator but left the dishes scattered over the table. They could wait for Wister. She knew that he'd wash them as soon as he came in because he hated any sort of mess lying around. She yawned and thought wearily that that was up to him. Nobody required him to wash dishes in the small hours of the morning. She turned out the light and left the kitchen, with Viter and Ed following close at her heels.

Wister had been standing just outside the kitchen door, waiting for them to leave. He had not wanted to come in while they were there. He did not know who Viter was and told himself that he did not care, either. He saw the mess of dishes on the table, compressed his lips, and began to carry them to the sink.

Maude went straight to her room, with Viter and Ed escorting her to the door. Her depression of the last few hours had lifted and she felt fairly sure that Una would get in touch with her in the morning.

Ed thought so too. He knew Una. She was flighty as hell and always doing crazy things.

Viter, having bowed Maude into her room, went to his own and was soon in bed. This Una woman would show up in the morning. As for the old man, he was probably a figment of Aloysius Graham's inebriation. There was the goatee, of course, but it didn't seem likely that it meant anything. The old man might have cut it off himself and buried it. Viter turned over and went to sleep at once.

Over in the left wing, Virginia was still wide awake. She could not sleep. She was much too excited, and even scared, and she thought, peevishly, that no one could sleep anyway, with Aloysius's snores screaming around the room.

She got up at last. There was no sense in just lying there, and anyway, she was hungry. She might as well get something to eat.

The lights were still burning in Aloysius's room and the downstairs hall, and she descended quietly, her hand gripping the banister nervously. In the lower hall she hesitated and then crept to the door that opened into the main part of the house. She pushed it ajar and peered through, but there was only darkness and silence, and she drew back with a little chill uncurling along her spine. She turned away, intent now on going straight upstairs again, but when she came to the living room she caught a glimpse of the bar and decided to make a sandwich as quickly as possible and take it up to bed with her.

She went in and turned on all the lights that would work. As she got out the bread and butter she realized that she'd better make two sandwiches, since Aloysius might wake up and would certainly want to share her snack if he did. Father, she thought impatiently as she prepared two sandwiches, could be brought out of a coma by the smell of food.

But this particular sandwich never got to Aloysius. Jim came in just as Virginia had halved it neatly with a carving knife and, seating himself at the bar, ate one of the halves in two bites.

"That was thoughtful of you," he said, eying her across the polished surface. "Getting up in the small hours of the morning and ministering to me like this. I may have a rugged exterior but those little attentions go straight to my heart. This sandwich was meant for me?"

Virginia nodded. "That's the one with the arsenic in it." She put her own sandwich onto the bar, came around and climbed onto a stool. She decided that she might as well eat downstairs, now that she had company.

Jim ate the other half of his sandwich in three bites and rattled the coffeepot to see if there was anything left in it. It swished encouragingly, so he put it on the grill and turned on the burner under it.

"Did they find Una?"

Virginia shook her head.

"What are they going to do about it?"

"As far as I can make out, they've all gone to bed."

Jim poured coffee, drank off a cupful, and felt in his pocket for cigarettes.

"I'm going to the police in the morning."

Virginia gave a wrenching yawn and muttered, "It's almost morning now."

He glanced at the windows behind them and saw that the darkness had gone gray. "So it is. Look, I want to go up to the attic to see if I can find out what frightened Susan. Will you come with me?"

"Why? Are you scared to go alone?"

"Certainly. Besides, these dark, silent hours seem to be the only times when we can have dates together." He stood up and, with a hand on her arm, urged her off the stool.

She went along, feeling too tired to protest, and asked almost feebly, "Is the girl business so bad that you have to chase after one who is reluctant?"

"You're not really reluctant," Jim said as they started up the stairs. "It's only the Graham feud that's holding you back. That and your old man, who is a stubborn, pigheaded old goat, even if he is my prospective father-in-law."

"Father's been called a lot of names in his time," Virginia said, stumbling against the banister in her weariness, "but to label him your prospective father-in-law is the worst yet. He'd never hold up his head again if he heard it."

There was gray light seeping in through the dusty attic windows and lying palely over a network of cobwebs. Old furniture, broken crockery, and battered books lay about under a film of dust, but nothing seemed to have been disturbed. They were nearly ready to go down again when they discovered a little old rocking chair with a man's new black leather slipper hanging precariously on its back.

CHAPTER 27

JIM LIFTED THE SLIPPER from the back of the little rocking chair and turned it over in his hands while Virginia watched him.

"Queer," he muttered, "it seems to be quite new. I wonder where the other one is."

He glanced around the dusty, cluttered attic and then stuffed the slipper into his pocket and began to search for its mate. Virginia continued to watch him for a while and eventually found herself searching along with him. They moved trunks, boxes, old pictures, chairs, and tables, and in one dark corner they came upon a roll of wire screening. Jim touched it with his foot and gave Virginia an accusing look.

"See that? Gathering dust in a Graham attic, when it is needed desperately by a lot of people who can't get it."

"Ant-and-grasshopper stuff," Virginia said, peering behind a trunk. "We Grahams have always saved money and been careful with our things, while you grasshopper Larsons spent your money on lights and tinsel. And then, when the lean time comes, people like you invariably have the immortal rind not to *ask* us to share but to *demand* it as your right. I'm sure—"

"All right," Jim said hastily. "I'd rather read it in book form."

They continued to search for some time but the only footgear that came to light was a pair of lady's green satin evening slippers. Jim held these objects up admiringly and observed that they looked as though champagne had been drunk out of them.

"Put them back," Virginia said tartly. "Although I can't blame you for being interested. I'm sure there's nothing half so gay in your Larson attics. Winter woolens in mothballs and old hymn books."

Jim replaced the shoes and dusted his hands. "Aren't you getting a little mixed up?" he asked mildly. "Green satin, champagne-holding evening slippers seem typical of a bunch of grasshopper Grahams, and certainly wool in mothballs and neatly stacked hymn books make a harmonious background for the Larson ants."

Virginia started to reply, got some dust in her throat, and coughed violently instead.

Jim said, "If you'll come over to the light, I'll have a look at that throat."

"Just keep out of my throat."

"Oh, all right, if you prefer to have Bert gawking into it." At this point the voice of Aloysius came thundering up the stairs.

"Who's up there?"

Virginia brushed ineffectually at her now dusty robe and started down the stairs, and Jim followed after a last glance around the attic.

Aloysius backed up hastily when he heard their descending footsteps but as soon as he saw them he advanced angrily.

"Where have you been? Waddya mean by going off and leaving me alone in your room with that girl Susan? How do you think that looks? Fine thing it would have been if she'd awakened and found herself alone there with me. Damned embarrassing all around."

"Don't flatter yourself, Father," Virginia said calmly. "Susan would merely have said, 'Can I get you a glass of water, Pop?' or something of that sort."

Aloysius winced and, after taking a moment to recover himself, launched into a different grievance.

"Now, wait a minute. I absolutely demand to know what you were doing in the attic with this man."

"Making love, of course," Virginia snapped, losing her temper.

Jim was shocked. "My dear, even in a joke, you shouldn't say a thing like that. When I make love to you, I shall do it decently, not in corners or up in attics."

"You mean you'll make love right out in the open, in front of everybody?"

"Certainly. In fact, now that your father is here, I'll give you a demonstration."

He took her hand, but Aloysius stepped over and slapped them apart.

"Keep your great farmer's hands off her. She wants nothing to do with you. She doesn't even like you."

"I don't believe it," Jim said carelessly.

"It's true!" Aloysius yelled. "D'ya think I'm a liar?"

Jim said, "Yes," and Virginia asked, "Did you leave Susan alone?"

"She's all right," Aloysius muttered impatiently. "Still asleep. Now look here, Jim Larson, my daughter is a cut above you socially and I don't intend—"

"What's your business phone number?" Jim asked Virginia. "I'm going to call them and say that you're ill and won't be in today."

"My daughter," said Aloysius, "has a position in life which—"

"I'll *have* to go in today. We're frightfully busy," Virginia sighed.

"You can't," Jim said flatly. "You need sleep and I, personally, am going to see that you get it. Give me that phone number."

"The Larsons," said Aloysius, "are, after all, only farmers of a coarse grain and you can't expect to make a silk purse out of a sow's ear."

"Oh, all right," Virginia said, "It's 674, but say that I'm coming in this afternoon because I am, even if I have to jump out of the window."

Jim nodded in agreement. "But go to bed right away. I don't think Susan will bother you. She'll probably be out until about noon now."

Virginia went into her bedroom and closed the door. Jim turned a chilly eye on Aloysius.

"You probably don't know this, Graham, but the Larsons are in direct descent from Queen Christina."

Aloysius was momentarily stumped. By the time a rejoinder occurred to him, Jim had gone downstairs and was making some breakfast at the bar. It was still very early and he wondered whether Jim had an eight o'clock operation at the hospital. It seemed probable, and Aloysius rubbed his hands together with satisfaction. Jim had been up most of the night and wasn't fit to operate. Perhaps he would damage the patient and be disgraced forever.

Now that the sun was coming into his room, he was no longer afraid, and he went in and lay down on the bed. The lamp had lost its eerie character and was just a utility. It made him think of Oliver P. and then of the two portraits. He decided again that the girls must have sold the original and had a copy made. The original must have been done by a name painter, though how could they sell it? Why would anyone want to buy it, name painter or not, with a puss like Oliver P.'s smeared over the canvas? At that, the painting made him much better-looking than he'd ever been in fact. Aloysius tried to remember Oliver P.'s living face and found his memory vague and confused. He'd seen so little of Oliver P. in the last twelve or fifteen years. Virginia had seen him, of course. He'd been quite fond of Virginia.

Suddenly, and quite clearly, he thought of P.X. Smith and opened his eyes wide. Smith's face had bothered him from the beginning with a nagging sense of familiarity. That was it, of course—he looked like Oliver P.

Aloysius sat up in bed. Maybe P.X. *was* Oliver P. And he was collecting the insurance, which was why the girls were so short of money. He thought back feverishly over P.X. Smith—his speech, his actions, every little thing he had done, and then the last sight he had had of him, sitting so still in that chair downstairs with his head battered and bloody.

Aloysius gasped and froze as he thought suddenly of a possible reason for the black goatee having been cut off P.X. Smith's face.

CHAPTER 28

ALOYSIUS SAID "Rubbish!" out loud and lay down again. He tried to put it all out of his mind and go to sleep, with the result that he found himself thinking furiously about it.

It was Una, of course, not Maude. Una had taken fright and run. She'd murdered her father so that she could collect the insurance for herself and then cut off his goatee to make sure of his identity. Just like Una, Aloysius thought, to feverishly murder the guy first and then shave his face to see if it was the guy.

But why should she disappear? She'd need to hang around to collect the insurance after all. Probably she intended to contact Maude, who would never give her away. She'd run because she was scared. That seemed to cover everything and he started from the beginning to think it all out carefully once more. But the sun was streaming in at his window now, and in that cheerful light he was inclined to characterize the whole thing as hogwash. It seemed likely that a much more simple explanation would turn up. In any case, he was tired and needed some sleep. He turned over and went off like a baby.

At about the same time Maude woke up and opened her eyes on a world that seemed dark with trouble. She dragged herself out of bed and went straight to the phone, where she called Bea. It was as she had expected. Bea was interested, sympathetic, and voluble, but she had not seen or heard from Una. Maude sat on the side of her bed and wondered rather helplessly what to do next. She'd have to wait, of course—she knew that—just wait until Una got in touch with her. But hers was not a passive nature and she simply could not sit around in a state of complete inactivity. She returned to the phone and called Bert.

She had to hold the instrument some inches away from her ear while Bert shrilled excitedly at her and announced, finally, that he would come over at once. Maude felt relief seeping through her for no particular reason and went downstairs to put on some coffee. On her way through the lower front hall she heard muffled coughing in the direction of the right wing and went at once to investigate.

It was Viter. He was arrayed in a robe of yellow silk brocade and was wiping his perspiring forehead with a matching handkerchief. Maude's hands went automatically, first to smooth her hair and then to pat at the folds of her own robe. It was a leftover from the days of plenty: an eggshell satin, rather severe in line and cut, and softened with fine beige lace at the neck. Maude gave the lace a hasty flip to hide a coffee stain as Viter smoothed his own hair and called a cheery good morning.

"I was thinking of searching this room again," he explained.

"You mean you don't trust Ed?"

"No, no, nothing of the sort," Viter said hastily. "But this room does not lend itself readily to amateur effort. It should be searched with professional care and I believe I'll go over it again."

"Well," Maude said, uninterested, "Ed took forever over it but I suppose you're right. Anyway, come and have some coffee first. Una's fiancé is coming over."

"Her fiancé?" Viter asked, raising his eyebrows. He felt a bit confused and wondered why the fiancé had not joined the search for Una during the previous night, especially since he lived just across the street.

Perhaps he'd been out on a case, Viter concluded. Yet Viter could not remember that anyone had ever bothered to notify him of Una's disappearance last evening while the ex-husband, who lived in the house, had searched long and valiantly. It was very peculiar.

"I suppose," said Viter aloud, "that he is very much distressed."

Maude nodded and held back, with difficulty, a comment on Bert's distress.

"Odd that he didn't come over last night."

"Oh, I didn't tell him," Maude explained. "Not until this morning. He's a doctor and needs his sleep, and anyway, she broke the engagement last night."

"Ah?"

"Yes," said Maude, heading for the kitchen and conscious that something bothered her with the soft nebulous insistence of a spider-web across her face. Something about the museum.

"Then why do you call him her fiancé?" Viter asked pleasantly.

"Oh well." Maude shrugged. There were so many things you might call Bert. Let him have his little hour as a fiancé She brought out cups and saucers and began to rattle them onto the table.

"At what time did she break the engagement?"

"As a matter of fact, I did it for her," Maude said, "when I had dinner with him last night."

"How did he take it?" Viter asked.

"Well enough. I suppose he thought it would be cheaper, anyhow."

"He's the type who is careful of his money?"

"That's one way of putting it," Maude agreed. "He coddles it, keeps it warm in the winter and cool in the summer."

Viter nodded and gave a passing thought to the fact that Maude was an entertaining personality as well as being handsome.

But Maude was not herself and she knew it. She brought the coffee to the table and sat down, but her eyes kept straying to the clock. Una was not an early riser at any time or under any circumstances, so that there seemed no hope of hearing from her before ten or eleven o'clock.

It seemed a long time to wait. Maude sipped at her coffee and continued to glance restlessly at the clock. Viter watched her with silent and unobtrusive admiration, and wondered whether something would come of the thought into which she seemed to be plunged.

Something did. She looked up suddenly, and said, "That light— the one in the museum. It shouldn't work. We threw the main switch for that wing a couple of weeks ago. The electric bill was too high, and we discovered we'd left the light burning in there for days on end. You can't see it from outside because the shutters are all closed and the door to the wing is edged with felt. That's why we didn't find out about the light for ages and then we threw the main switch to prevent it happening again."

"Then someone turned that switch on sometime before we made our search last night."

Maude nodded. "I used that light first last night. I'd forgotten about having thrown the main switch, and I went in there to hunt for Una's suitcase, which I found immediately, as you know."

"Yes. Had you and your sister left that suitcase where you found it?"

"No," Maude said thoughtfully. "We stacked all those suitcases carefully in the closet, with the small ones on top. Una's was a very small one, so that it must have been right on top. Someone had moved it."

Viter closed his eyes and imagined Una pulling the little suitcase down from the top of the pile and standing it on the floor, and then, nothing. It was blank from there on. She did not use it and she had not packed her clothes in anything else. She just didn't seem to have done anything after that.

Maude gave a small exclamation, and he opened his eyes.

"Something kept bothering me about that museum," she said, "and I couldn't exactly place it, but I remember now. It was when I went to look for Una's suitcase. The lid was off one of those coffins."

CHAPTER 29

MAUDE HAD GONE RATHER white. Viter, after a glance at her, stood up abruptly. "Come, Mrs. Watson, we shall go and have a look."

Maude followed him slowly. "But it's on now—the lid, I mean. It's back on again."

"It may have been a trick of your excited imagination," Viter said soothingly. "You have been worried and upset, you know."

Maude shook her head. "No, no, I remember distinctly now, the lid was off and leaning against the coffin, and then later it was on again. It's been bothering at my mind but I couldn't remember exactly. Oh God, I hope it isn't—"

Her voice trailed off and Viter turned back and took her arm comfortably in his. "Come, now, we shall look at once and have it off our minds." He marched her over to where the three coffins stood in a row and asked, "Which one?"

Maude touched the first in line and whispered, "That one." Her teeth were chattering and she ground them together in an effort to stop it.

Viter stepped forward, and found that the lid came off easily and was not very heavy. He peered around it and was disappointed to find that the box was empty, although he had self-control enough to give Maude an encouraging smile. "You see? All that hand-wringing for nothing."

Maude relaxed with a long sigh and felt that the blood was moving through her body again after having been suspended for a while.

Viter leaned over and examined the inside of the coffin very carefully. There appeared to be nothing but he ran his hand over the smooth surface because he knew that his eyes were no longer as sharp as they had been. It was annoying and irritating but it had to be faced. He often missed small objects now and he couldn't always be pulling out his reading glasses, especially with a handsome woman like Maude around.

His fingers touched a small object, and he knew without looking that it was a bobby pin. He glanced at Maude but she had not noticed anything, and he felt that he could not tell her, at least not now. She seemed to have recovered completely and was lighting a cigarette.

"I suppose I got into a bit of a panic," she said, exhaling a long, thin stream of smoke. "Let my imagination run away with me."

Viter nodded and closed his hand around the bobby pin. The women seemed to use the things more than hairpins these days In fact, he had seen some who let their hair dangle like the head of a mop, without any anchorage at all. He thought of his mother, who had used a round dozen tortoiseshell hairpins and three combs to keep her hair pinned to her head, and shrugged his shoulders. Times certainly changed. Well, he must find an opportunity to go to Una's bedroom and see whether he could match the bobby pin.

They went back to the kitchen and Maude chattered volubly in a reaction from nervousness. She decided that she had been making a fuss about nothing and that Una would certainly get in touch with her before long. She began to clatter the dishes over to the sink. Viter was torn between a gallant desire to help her and a feeling that now was his opportunity to go to Una's bedroom. In the end, he convinced himself that business must come before pleasure and said to Maude, "Excuse me for just a moment. I'm going upstairs but I'll be right down to dry the dishes for you."

"Of course," Maude said brightly. "Only, I can manage this by myself."

She supposed vaguely that he was making for the bathroom, and she nearly called out that there was a downstairs lavatory and then decided that he might be embarrassed.

Viter went straight to Una's room and straight to the top drawer of the bureau, since that's where his mother and his deceased wife had always kept their hairpins.

There were no bobby pins in the drawer but he found letters, several stacks of them. He glanced around the room and saw that there was a desk, and yet the woman kept letters in her top bureau drawer. He looked rapidly through three or four and found that they were love letters, some of them with recent dates. It was a break, he thought, and he'd have to make an opportunity to read them all through carefully. He closed the drawer and continued the search for bobby pins.

There was a mirrored dressing table, skirted in flowing pink taffeta, and as he approached it he saw that the taffeta was soiled and torn. They were not keeping the place up. That was very obvious. But he found the bobby pins and compared them with the one in his hand. Some were like it and some were not. That was the trouble with these bobby pins. His mother's tortoiseshell hairpins had had much more individuality. Still, there were some in the dressing table like the one in his hand. And Maude had seen the lid off that coffin

Viter scratched his chin and looked into space. It was one of those things, a murderer who was most anxious to hide his victims but changed his mind about where to hide them. Evidently he'd found a good place in the end, and Viter felt impelled to find that place before the bodies were destroyed altogether.

He went downstairs again. Maude was putting away the clean dishes while Bert sat at a table, staring with haggard eyes at a cup of coffee. As a matter of fact, Bert didn't drink coffee as a rule. He didn't think it was good for him, but Maude never could seem to remember it and was always pushing it at him. He took occasional sips at the cup that steamed before him now because he didn't want to waste it, nor did he want to offend Maude.

Maude introduced him to Viter but made no explanation beyond saying, "Mr. Viter is staying with us."

Bert nodded and fell to wondering why Maude opened up her house to so many guests when food and service were so frightfully expensive. He thought of the guest rooms in his own house and resolved to have all of them locked up. It would keep them in better condition and then, when prices went down, he could perhaps open them up and have a guest or two now and then.

Maude was saying, "I think Una will be getting in touch with me at any time now."

Bert nodded absently and took another sip of coffee. Viter, who had taken a tray of clean dishes from Maude and was putting them away in the wrong places, said, "Why don't you take a couple of aspirins, Mrs. Watson, and try to get a little extra sleep? If the phone rings, I shall wake you at once."

Bert glanced up at her. "You really should, Maude. You look very tired. I have some aspirin here. I'll give you one. One should be enough."

"I think I shall," Maude said, after a glance at the clock.

To Bert's horror, she took three aspirin tablets, and, seeing the shock reflected in his face, she explained, "I always have to have three or I get no results."

"But you don't have a headache," Bert protested, trying to save at least one of his tablets. "And you don't need three just to relax you."

"It's the same thing with cocktails," Maude said, washing down the three tablets with a glass of water. "Never feel the first two but the third always starts my tongue wagging at both ends."

Bert watched gloomily until the aspirin had gone beyond recall, and then he took a final swallow of coffee and stood up.

"You will let me know immediately when you have heard from Una?"

Maude said she would let him know without delay, if she had to push her way into the delivery room to do it, and Bert frowned, colored, and took himself off, murmuring that he was due at the hospital.

Maude poured coffee for herself and Viter and sat down at the table.

"I drink this stuff all day," she said idly. "If it were alcohol, I'd be an alcoholic."

Viter smiled at her. "You'll lie down when you've finished that cup, won't you? You really need rest."

He felt a genuine concern for her fatigue, but he was also anxious to go through the love letters as well and he wanted her out of the way.

Maude nodded. "I might as well, I'm tired enough."

But she made no move to go and Viter was afraid to urge her too much. His mind began to fidget with ways and means. Ed came bursting into the kitchen with his hair rumpled and his eyes sparkling with excitement.

"Maudie, you've been robbed! All your money is gone!"

CHAPTER 30

MAUDE LOOKED UP, her face pinching again in alarm, and asked, "What money, Ed? What's eating you? Has the bank failed?"

Ed deflated a trifle and tried to smooth his hair into some semblance of order. "No, not the bank. Maybe you took that money out yourself, Maudie?"

"Sit down and have a cup of coffee," Maude said sensibly, "and explain yourself."

Ed sat down, still working abstractedly on his hair. "I suppose you did take it yourself, but it was a crazy place to keep it, Maude. The bank's much safer. Suppose there was a fire? That flimsy wooden cabinet would go up like a pine tree. Ever see a pine tree burn? Disappears in a puff of smoke."

"Suppose we leave the discussion of pine trees for a more social moment," Viter said sternly. "What cabinet were you referring to and where is it?"

Ed, suddenly cautious, sent Viter a wary glance and devoted himself to his coffee. He began to wish fervently that he had not mentioned the money in front of Viter. It would have been much smarter to wait until he had Maude alone. A guy like Viter could always put two and two together and find out that Ed had gone to the cabinet to borrow a five. There might be a certain amount of difficulty in getting him to understand that the five was to have been merely a loan until Ed received the check he was expecting. Ed was no thief. He had never stolen a nickel in his life. Besides, it certainly couldn't have harmed anyone for him to have borrowed a five out of that drawer for a few days. But it was hard to explain that to a cold proposition like Viter. Ed wished, with a long sigh, that someone had taught him at an impressionable age to hold his tongue.

"To what cabinet were you referring?" Viter asked inexorably.

Ed sighed again. "In the museum—a Chinese cabinet there. It was when I was searching last night. In one of the drawers of this cabinet I found hundreds of dollars and I thought that was where Maudie kept a reserve fund of some sort. I was interested in the cabinet, you understand—most interesting old piece—and that's how I came to be opening the drawers. Now, what's worrying me, I went there this morning, just wanted to look over the cabinet again, it being a very fascinating old piece, er, well—" His voice trailed off as he tried to think of some plausible excuse for having opened the drawer again but since nothing occurred to him he finished rather lamely, "Well, anyway, the money was gone."

Viter stood up at once and said, "Show me the cabinet, please, and the drawer," and Ed made for the right wing, wondering all the way why he was not only taking orders but obeying them like a blasted mouse.

Maude followed them indifferently. She supposed Ed had been drinking too much and had imagined the whole thing.

But Viter had been putting two and two together, just as Ed had feared. He was sure that Ed had returned to the cabinet to borrow five, ten, or a hundred, with the cheerful intention of putting it back later, because he knew Ed.

However, he kept this mathematical calculations to himself and merely asked Maude if she were sure that Una had not kept some money in the drawer.

Maude denied it emphatically. She could account for all of her own money, as well as Una's, and certainly none of it had been in a drawer of the Chinese cabinet.

"But it must have been thousands," Ed declared.

"Nonsense!" Maude said, and added almost immediately, "Or wait a minute. Perhaps it belonged to Wister. I know he has plenty, and he might have decided to take it out of the bank and hide it in the house. He gets some odd ideas in his straitlaced head at times."

Viter wasted no time in speculation, but went straight to Wister's room and woke him up. He asked rather peremptorily about the money, but Wister replied tersely that any money in the house belonging to him was reposing in his wallet and nowhere else. He further went on to inquire, courteously but coldly, who Viter was and what his business might be.

"I am a special investigator," Viter said with dignity, "and I have been called in to clear up certain mysterious happenings in the house. I should be very glad of your help and cooperation, if you would care to give it."

Wister, still a bit chilly, said he'd be glad to help in any way he could but that since he was ignorant of any and all mysterious happenings, he thought he should be enlightened.

However, Viter decided against enlightening anyone who might be a suspect and merely observed that it was just as well he'd been called in, because of the Mrs. Randall development.

Wister's attitude changed at once and he asked quickly, "What is it? What has happened to Mrs. Randall?"

"Do you know where she is?"

"I?" Wister asked, his voice suddenly shrill. "What do you mean?"

"Have you any idea where she has gone?"

"She has gone somewhere?"

"Yes," said Viter, "she has gone somewhere and she did not take a suitcase or any personal belongings."

Wister began to ask questions, rapid, abrupt questions which annoyed Viter with the feeling that their status as investigator and family retainer had been reversed. He was about to point this out with emphasis when Wister dismissed him from the bedroom. Viter got out and then stood in the kitchen for a moment, wondering just where and how he had lost control of the situation.

"What did he say?" Maude asked.

"Nothing," Viter said briefly.

"Was it his money?" Ed asked curiously.

Viter looked offended and said, "I wouldn't know. We never got that far. He put me out."

Maude laughed. Viter turned to her and urged her to a seat at the table. He sat down opposite her, folded his arms on the edge of the table, and said, "Now tell me about Wister. You said that he was the butler, or houseman, or some such thing, but I can see that there's something more. You'd better tell me."

Maude frowned down at the fingers of her right hand, which were drumming on the table, and Ed, watching them both, decided that he didn't want to be bored with Wister's life history. He was hungry, too, since Maude had offered him nothing beyond the one cup of coffee. He didn't blame her. Ed thought she'd been worried and upset, but just the same, a cup of coffee didn't hold a guy for very long. He left the kitchen quietly and made for the left wing.

He found Aloysius, Virginia, and Susan dressed for the day and holding a conference.

"Mrs. Anderson will give us something," Aloysius was saying. "The Kuntree Koffee Shoppe doesn't open until eleven-thirty and I can't wait that long. I may look like a strong, husky fella, but I need plenty of nourishing food to keep going, especially after the hard night I had. I can't let you two decent girls go to that dirty diner and the drugstore isn't serving food this week because Willie is away on vacation."

"We could get some supplies in town and bring them back here," Virginia said, giving her parent a cold eye.

"What's the matter?" Ed asked. "Run out of food?"

"Mr. Graham forgot to do the marketing yesterday," Susan explained, avoiding Aloysius's choleric eye, "so we have nothing for breakfast and we don't like to bother Mrs. Watson—"

"Wouldn't help you anyway," Ed said cheerfully. "Maudie's upset and she forgot to give me anything except a cup of coffee. But Wishy has the right idea. We'll go over to Bert's and get this Mrs. Whosis to feed us. Splendid idea. You can always count on Wishy to save the day." He caught Virginia's arm and said, "Come on, sugar, let's go. Bert won't know anything about it because he's over at the hospital making grave fodder."

He walked her through to the main house and out the front door, while Aloysius and Susan followed on behind. Virginia protested the entire way, but Ed merely patted her shoulder and explained that a young thing of her years should defer to the judgment of a man of the world like himself. At one point she declared that it was dishonest to eat a man's food behind his back. Ed was astounded.

"Why, baby," he said, "that's the only way you ever could eat Bert's food. If you tried to eat it in front of him, he'd put his hand right in your mouth, get it out again, and put it back in the refrigerator to await the next stew."

As Aloysius had predicted, Mrs. Anderson was glad to see them. She was fond of company and she loved to talk. She sat them around the kitchen while she prepared a sumptuous breakfast. Aloysius tried to help her but she pushed him away, prattling cheerfully all the time. She laughed heartily over their predicament, and when the meal was ready, she sat down and ate with them. No one gave this a thought except Aloysius, who was old enough to remember the old master-and-servant regime, and he treated her with excessive courtesy to show her that he didn't mind.

At the height of the bonhomie, Mr. Anderson walked in and said sharply, "Cut it out, cut it out, you want the police and fire department here? Didn't you know Doc came home with his leg in a sling?"

"Merciful heavens!" Mrs. Anderson exclaimed, pleasurably excited, and hoping for the worst. "Where is he? What happened to him?"

"He's in bed," said Mr. Anderson. "Me and Doc Larson carried

him there. He got knocked down by a car. Doc Larson thinks his
ankle's busted."

CHAPTER 31

THERE WAS AN OUTBURST of exclamations and Mr. Anderson
hushed them sharply again.

"Anybody coulda heard youse a mile away," he said severely.
"The only reason Doc didn't hear nothing was because he was hollering
to raise the dead himself."

"Why didn't they take him to the hospital?" Aloysius asked in a
hoarse whisper.

"He's afraida that butcher shop," Mr. Anderson explained simply.
"Seen too many of his patients goin' outta there feet first."

Jim appeared at the kitchen door, saying, "Are you deaf?" and
then stopped short and eyed the assemblage. "What is it—a board
meeting?"

"Breakfast party," Virginia said briefly.

He gave her a fleeting grin and then turned to Susan. "Give me a
hand, will you? He won't go to the hospital and have an X-ray but I
think it's only a sprain, anyway. I'm going to strap it up."

Susan jumped up and said, "Sure. Shall I run over and change
into uniform?"

"No, come on up as you are. How do you feel?"

"I'm just fine," Susan said cheerfully.

He wrinkled his forehead at her. "I though you'd be out cold until
about noon."

"Not me," Susan declared, carelessly. "Drugs never hold me for
very long. Being in the business, as you might say, I've always taken
them when I had a pain or needed sleep, so now I'm kind of used to
them."

Jim wanted to lecture her severely on this loose attitude in regard
to drugs but Bert was groaning loudly upstairs and he had a busy
morning before him, so he decided to postpone it and merely hoped
that he wouldn't forget about it.

He took Susan upstairs and announced casually to Bert, "I ran across my office nurse, so I brought her along to help."

"You ran across her?" Bert asked, lifting his head from the pillow and then dropping it back again with a groan.

"He saw me through the window," Susan explained with a sunny smile. "I had just stopped in the driveway to admire your lovely garden. It's simply wonderful. I don't know how you get all those different flowers together in one spot without them quarreling. Then Dr. Larson saw me and called me in."

Bert was slightly mollified but he turned to Jim and asked suspiciously, "Why did you go to the front window? You wanted some things from my office and I told you that was at the back of the house."

Jim gave Susan a glance that despaired of her intellect and said shortly, "I wanted to look at the garden, too. I thought I heard a spat between the pansies and the iris."

They went to work on the injured ankle, and Bert, between occasional sharp cries of pain, suggested that no really conscientious doctor would waste time looking at a garden when he was on a case. "Those few stolen moments," he declaimed, gaining momentum, "might be the critical period that decides the life or death of the patient."

"Well, you were lucky," Jim said, finishing with the ankle and handing Bert a capsule and a glass of water with which to wash it down. "You passed the crisis all alone up here, while I refereed for a couple of blooms, and damn, you're going to recover. You have my professional word on it."

Bert gave him an evil look but Jim ignored it and went on down to the kitchen, where he found Mrs. Anderson telling a story of her girlhood in Sweden.

"It wasn't as though I'd been a small girl," she was saying, with a downward glance at her present ample curves. "I was a big, husky young thing, twice as big as him, and yet I had to have a chaperon to protect me from him."

"Maybe they insisted on the chaperon as a protection to him," Jim suggested.

Mrs. Anderson gave a loud appreciative shriek and laughed herself into hiccups. When she had recovered sufficiently to wipe her eyes and become articulate, she asked, "How's Doc? Do I have to go sit with him?"

Jim shook his head. "Just look in on him from time to time and see whether he wants anything. I expect he'll be pretty cross."

"Never saw him any other way," Mrs. Anderson declared without venom. "Have a cup of coffee, Doc."

"No, thanks. I'd like to but I haven't time. I've some of Dr. Hanson's calls to make, as well as my own. I'll be off, then, and if that ankle kicks up too much, get in touch with me."

Mrs. Anderson nodded. On his way out, Jim brushed past Aloysius and whispered something into Virginia's ear.

Aloysius at once rose up in wrath and yelled, "What did he say? Why do you let him get so familiar with you? What is it he said?"

"Perfect reaction," Virginia sighed "He wanted to get your goat and he walked off with it under his arm."

Mrs. Anderson looked from one to the other of them, her eyes round with astonishment. "You don't favor a match between your daughter and the young doctor?" she asked Aloysius.

"I'll twist his nose off and ram it down his throat first," Aloysius raved.

"But he's doing well and he's a fine young man. You should help your daughter capture him. It isn't easy to get a husband these days and you should be careful not to drive the young man away."

Aloysius was momentarily shocked into silence. Virginia, after an amused glance at him, kindly explained it to Mrs. Anderson.

"Those were just tactics. Very often the young men are apt to run, if the parents are too eager. Father has frightened off several prospects in that way, so he hopes to catch this one by playing hard to get."

Mrs. Anderson nodded her head rather doubtfully but sent a look at Aloysius which was full of admiration for his courage. He glared back at her, sputtered savagely at Virginia, and then stamped out the back door, slamming it loudly behind him.

Ed had drawn Susan into a corner and was making up to her in a slightly outdated but thoroughly easy fashion when the slam of the back door interrupted him. He asked, "What's that?" in a startled voice but nobody bothered to tell him.

Virginia had begun to clear away the dishes, and Mrs. Anderson, busy at the sink, kept telling her not to bother. Virginia continued to help, but Mrs. Anderson was not too concerned until Ed picked up a dish towel. Then she became really upset. She felt that it was not for a gentleman like Mr. Randall to be doing menial work in her kitchen. She did not breathe easily until the dishes were done and she was able to show him and Susan out the back door.

Virginia leaned against the kitchen table, lit a cigarette, and smoked it moodily. Mrs. Anderson, after a glance at the dock, murmured, "I guess I'll go up and see if Doc wants anything."

Virginia yawned. "I'll go with you. I'll tell him I came over especially to see him."

They went upstairs but as they approached Bert's room he began a series of loud, querulous complaints, so that Virginia decided to postpone her visit, and Mrs. Anderson went in alone.

"I could be dying here," Bert moaned, "and none of you would concern yourselves. Everyone goes off and leaves me lying helpless on my bed with not so much as a cup of tea brought to me. Here, hand me those two canes. You'll have to help me to the bathroom."

Virginia, just outside the door, heard the uproar as Bert was helped out of bed and decided that she'd better make herself scarce. She tried two doors in succession along the hall, found them both locked, and at last, in a bit of a panic, slipped into a small room that contained a studio couch, a sewing machine, two straight chairs, and a table. It was next to the bathroom. She pulled the door to but left a crack through which she watched Bert's slow and painful advance. He kept the bad foot off the floor entirely and hopped along, with the aid of his two canes, while Mrs. Anderson hovered from side to side, pretending to help. She became so irritating, at last, that Bert sent her off in a fury.

He had almost reached the bathroom when he noticed that the door to the sewing room was not quite closed and he hesitated, frowning. He had had all the guest rooms locked up but this sewing room connected with one of them through a closet and it ought to be locked up too. No sewing was ever done there, anyway.

The key was in the lock, on the outside of the door, and Bert hopped over painfully, closed the door, and turned the key firmly in the lock.

CHAPTER 32

BERT PUT THE KEY to the sewing room into his pocket and hopped into the bathroom. He tried, tentatively, to put the injured foot to the floor but the pain was very bad and he raised it again with a groan. But there was no fracture. He felt sure of that. Larson might need an X-ray to be certain on that point but an older man like himself had more experience. These young fools had to have all sorts of tests and gadgets to back up a diagnosis. If the machine were out of order, then the diagnosis was out of order too. Couldn't depend on their own minds. Larson certainly couldn't because he didn't have a mind. Always joking and cutting up, even if the patient were in agony. It was an utter disgrace.

Bert had a suspicion that he was thinking foolishly, which put him in a worse temper than ever. He knew that he should have gone to the hospital, where he could have been cared for properly, but he had wanted to come home. He'd never been a patient in a hospital and it didn't appeal to him now. Not that he was afraid, of course, but he just wasn't used to it.

He made his way back from the bathroom a little more easily than he had got there, putting the injured foot down once or twice despite the pain. He thought angrily that he should have had an extra bathroom put in when he had the wings added. The master bedroom should have its own bath. It was the expense which had deterred him. He should have had it done, as the architect had wanted. It would have made a vast difference to him just now in convenience.

By the time he got back to bed the pain was very bad. He lay back and closed his eyes, hoping that he could sleep, but instead of relaxing, he found that his mind was racing furiously. He'd have to wait until Mrs. Anderson came back before he could get another capsule. He'd never be able to sleep without one. He took a book from the bedside table and tried to read but it was impossible. Most of the words would not focus and even when they did, he could make no sense out of them. He was ghastly tired, exhausted to the point of tears, and yet he could not sleep.

Virginia, imprisoned in the sewing room, was wondering what she ought to do. She had backed away from the door when Bert locked her in, too embarrassed to reveal herself. She was due at the office directly after lunch and had a hundred things to do, anyhow. And here she was, with not so much as a book to pass the time away. She decided, in the end, to wait until she heard Mrs. Anderson in the hall and then to knock quietly on the door. Fortunately for her peace of mind, she did not know that Bert had put the key into the pocket of his bathrobe.

She lit a cigarette and then discovered that there was not a single ashtray in the room. She used a small vase at last, wondering idly why it was not filled with flowers, since there were so many in the garden. She lay down on the studio couch and wondered uneasily why Mrs. Anderson did not come back. Surely Bert must be asking for service again by this time.

She stretched comfortably and realized that she was tired. She had wanted to sleep through until it was time to go to work but Susan had roused early and when Susan was awake, nobody could sleep in the same room with her because she prattled without ceasing. Virginia yawned and decided that she could go to sleep right now, if she'd let herself. But there was so much to do, and she'd have to listen for Mrs. Anderson. She closed her eyes, telling herself that she could hear better that way, and went to sleep at once.

Susan did not notice that Virginia had disappeared because she was chatting gaily with Ed. She knew that Gus would not approve, if he could see her, but she was quite sure that there was no harm in it. They were both having a good time, and she hated to break it up, but she knew that she ought to change into her uniform and get down to the office. She'd have to confer with Miss Hall, Dr. Hanson's office nurse, about what cases it would be necessary for Jim to take over. Miss Hall worked only in the afternoon, which made it cheaper for Dr. Hanson.

"I'll have to tell her," Susan explained to Ed, "that Jim can take only the urgent cases. Poor Jim, he really will be rushed today."

"Oh, nuts," Ed said easily. "Leave us not worry about J. Larson's troubles. Serves him right for being so shortsighted as to pick out such a business for himself. Now me, when I take a vacation, I really relax. Nothing on my mind but spiderwebs."

He laughed heartily. Susan laughed with him but rather to his surprise, she was quite firm about changing into her uniform and getting down to work.

He said good-by to her reluctantly and then, after only a short moment of indecision, sought out Aloysius. The two of them thereupon, and without words at all, made their way to the left wing and mixed some drinks.

Maude appeared after a while and looked them over with a worldly-wise eye. She sank into a chair and said tiredly, "I knew I'd find you here. Mix me a stiff one, will you?"

They supplied her promptly and she downed the drink in a hurry and asked for another. It was almost noon now and there had been no word from Una. She didn't expect to hear from her any more. It seemed certain that something had happened to her right here in the house. P.X. Smith had been killed, their own father, and Una had been killed too. But why? What was behind it all? And there was all the money that Ed had seen in the Chinese cabinet. Why was it there and why hadn't Father used it? He had no other money to live on. It was odd that she and Una had not discovered it earlier. God knows, they could have used it. But Una was gone and would never have a chance of using it now. She had always badly wanted money. Of course that money might have belonged to Wister. It was possible that he had hidden it there and had removed it this morning. Only Wister was the type who believed in banks or safe stocks and bonds. He had always said so. He was not a miser who delighted in running his hands through actual money. He liked neat piles of gilt-edged bonds and bankbooks recording substantial sums.

Maude sighed heavily and drained the dregs of her second drink.

Viter peered in at her and, after a brief hesitation, withdrew again. He would have liked to go and sit with her but he had work to do and he was conscientious about the business of work before pleasure.

He had a theory that people always left traces of themselves and if you looked hard enough, you could find them. He was convinced that Una had been in that coffin and he had been all over the back garden trying to pick up her trail. He was ready, now, to do the front garden.

It was tedious work, but he felt that it would pay off. That slipper, now, that had been found hanging on the rocking chair in the left wing—it must have belonged to the man Smith. Smith's body had been carried out of the attic and that was how the slipper had caught on the chair. Later the murderer had come back to look for the slipper and had run into Susan, and screamed. Hysterical—and why not? Probably he had mistaken Susan for Una, and he had just murdered Una. No wonder he screamed.

Viter had reached the road by this time, and almost immediately his search was rewarded. He found a bobby pin. It was identical with the one that had been in the coffin.

CHAPTER 33

VITER PICKED UP the bobby pin and looked at it carefully. But there wasn't much, he thought regretfully, to be learned from such a small object. It was just a bobby pin. Certainly it was shiny and new looking, indicating that it had been dropped recently, but unfortunately the world was peopled with women who went around dropping bobby pins. It might or might not have come from Una's sleek black head. He sighed and put it into his pocket. Anyway, he thought, his face brightening, he had earned a rest, and Maude drew him like a magnet. He turned around and made his way back to the left wing.

Maude looked up at once, when he came in, searching his face for news, but he avoided her anxious eyes. There was nothing that he could tell her, at least nothing of any consequence. Maude saw the evasion and handed her glass to Ed for another drink.

Viter cleared his throat and swept them with a glance. "We must find out more about this P.X. Smith and, if possible, contact his family. Have you no idea where he came from?"

"Down South somewhere," Aloysius said shortly. He was jealous of Viter and had a longing to make a monkey out of him. He had discovered that Ed felt exactly the same way.

Viter nodded. "Yes, I see. Now what hotel was he staying at before he came here?"

"*The* hotel," Aloysius said disgustedly. "What do you think this is, New York or something? There's one hotel in the village and that's where he was staying."

"Quite so. I shall go there for lunch. I should be able to find out where Smith hailed from by looking at the hotel register."

"You're not going to like it much," Ed warned him. "The food's terrible."

"What do you mean?" Aloysius demanded. "It's the only place you can get food that's fit to eat."

Ed made a face. "Slops. Tearoom stuff—creamed chipped beef on toast, and no bar. That's the Kuntree Koffee Shoppe."

"Come on," Aloysius said to Viter, "I'll go down with you. The hotel doesn't run a restaurant but this Kuntree Koffee Shoppe has an entrance from the lobby and all the guests use it. Go and get your hat, Maude."

"I haven't worn a hat in three years," Maude said tartly. "Go and get your own hat. You need one in this weather or the top of your head will get sunburned."

But Maude didn't go with them, in the end. She was afraid to leave the house for fear Una would try to contact her. Viter, gallantly thoughtful for her welfare, ordered Ed to stay with her. He would have liked to get rid of Aloysius, too, but there seemed no tactful way to accomplish it, so he made the best of it. He was silent for a while as they walked toward the village, and then he said abruptly, "Mr. Graham, I cannot believe that this P.X. Smith was an absolute stranger to all of you. Are you quite sure that you know nothing whatever about him?"

It had always been said of Aloysius, from infancy on, that he was unable to keep his mouth shut, and he now found this grave invitation to confidence beyond his power to resist. He unburdened himself of what he knew about Oliver P. Graham, P.X. Smith, and the uncanny resemblance between the two, if there *were* two.

"It didn't strike me at first," Aloysius said earnestly, "because that old goat, Oliver P., and I were not on speaking terms for some years before he died and I hadn't seen so much of him. But when it finally hit me, I wondered how I'd missed it."

"But you say Oliver P. Graham never wore a goatee, and this man did?"

"Yes, but that may be why I didn't notice it sooner. Another thing, old Oliver P. never went gray, his hair was black, and although this P.X. Smith was quite elderly, his hair was black too and so was the goatee."

"Perhaps that was the only resemblance," Viter said doubtfully. "They were both old men and both had black hair."

Aloysius frowned and shook his head in a bothered way. "I don't know, it was just the general look of him." He went on to air his theory that P.X. Smith was actually Oliver P. and had been collecting the insurance money while the girls went short. Viter listened with such absorbed interest that he entered the Kuntree Koffee Shoppe, sat down and ordered something, and didn't come to until he found himself eating mackerel, which had always been his pet abomination. But Aloysius, now wound up and unable to stop, was undoubtedly interesting. He went on to give details and anecdotes of the Graham family life that Viter ordinarily would not have been able to pick up in the course of several years. He said nothing about Wister having been one of Una's beaux, simply because he did not know of it.

Ed was more relieved than anything else at being left with Maude, since he disliked both unnecessary exertion and the food at the Kuntree Koffee Shoppe. "Two slices of beet on a piece of wilted lettuce is their idea of a salad, Maudie. Now, I'll make you a real salad for lunch and all you'll have to do is to sit down and fold your hands until it's ready."

As a matter of fact, it didn't work out that way, since Ed was obliged to call for assistance early on in the proceedings. In the end, Maude found that she was preparing the lunch, while Ed got in her way from time to time.

In the midst of the confusion, Wister came out of his room, carefully dressed and brushed, and said courteously to Maude, "Good day. Where is Una?"

Ed goggled at him and Maude looked up in slight confusion. She frowned at Wister, wiped her hands on a paper towel, and at last said firmly, "Una has disappeared, as I think Mr. Viter told you. I was hoping you'd know something about it. And I wanted to ask you about some money in that Chinese—"

"Disappeared?" Wister interrupted. "Mr., er, Viter said something about her having gone off, but surely you know where she is?"

"No, I don't!" Maude said sharply. She told him the details of Una's disappearance. When he earnestly disclaimed any knowledge of the affair, she left it wearily and asked him about the money in the Chinese cabinet.

He drew back a step and gave her a chilly look. "I know nothing of any money in this house, except that which is now on my own person, and rightfully so. My savings are in the bank."

"What about those hundred-dollar bills you were seen handling?" Maude asked, losing patience with him.

He colored slightly and his eyes dropped. "I was taking care of them for a friend."

"What friend? Maude demanded. "Una, perhaps?"

He turned to go without a word but Maude stamped her foot and called imperiously, "Wister, you come back here at once! I'm not going to stand for your petty tantrums any longer."

Wister stopped and turned slowly, his sullen eyes on Maude's face, and she added sharply, "Una has disappeared and it's time you stopped skulking around with a lot of little secrets hidden under your hat. Una *must* be found, and I think the first step is for you to open up and tell me what you know."

Wister said almost mildly, "She will surely turn up soon, because we—"

Maude said in a voice of deadly seriousness, "Get this—it's important. Una was going to start a new life altogether. She had no intention of coming back to any of her old companions."

There was a moment's silence, and then Wister said quietly, "I see."

His face was blank but behind it his mind raced furiously. He wanted to get away from Maude but he was a little afraid of her in: her present mood.

"I think you'd better tell me where you got those hundred dollar bills," she said flatly.

Wister gave a short sigh and said without any noticeable emotion,

"It was the money that you and Una left every month in the attic for your father."

"Do you know who collected that money?"

"Yes," said Wister, "I know. I didn't see why he should get it, so I took it myself to hold for you."

"Do you mean that P.X. Smith—no, Father—came for it every month?"

"You're a little confused about that P.X Smith," Wister said. "Although there is a definite resemblance, he very definitely is not your father."

CHAPTER 34

MAUDE LEANED AGAINST the wall with a feeling of utter despair. Her father was still alive and she and Una would continue to be without funds. I'll expose him, she thought wildly, and go and get a job. But I won't live like that ever again.

Ed whispered, "My God, Maude! What is he talking about? Your father died years ago."

Maude hardly heard him. Wister had turned and was making quietly for the back door and she could see that he was desperate to get away from her. She pulled herself together and called sharply, "Wait a minute. How do you know that Smith was not Father?"

Wister looked at her and became a butler again without either of them noticing it. "Miss Maude, I knew every line of your father's face. He would not have anyone shave him but me and although it was not my place, I indulged him. I shaved him every morning for many years and I could never mistake his face. I'm not denying the resemblance but Mr. Smith is not your father."

"You knew Father was still living?"

"I knew all about it, Miss Maude. I knew why you put that money in the left wing each month and when Mr. Smith appeared, I had the same thought that you did about him. But as soon as I saw him at close range, I knew that he was not your father."

"Was it Father himself who picked up the money each month?" Maude asked.

"No, it was not. I have seen it going on for many months, and I wanted to interfere because it was a very wrong thing, Miss Maude. You know that. But I did not dare to do anything until this month and then I just went to the attic myself and picked it up and put it away. Blackmail is an evil thing and you and your sister had suffered long enough."

"So you put the money in that Chinese cabinet in the right wing," Ed supplied interestedly.

Wister gave him a cold stare and said, "I did nothing of the kind. I put it in a special savings account in the bank."

"Nobody seems to worry about that money in the cabinet," Ed muttered, shaking his head. "Nobody seems to care, but I tell you there were thousands and it's all gone."

"You were tight, Ed," Maude said impatiently, and turned again to Wister. "What did you do, wait around and spy on the person who came for the money?"

"Yes, Miss Maude, I did."

"I don't suppose you knew him, anyway," Maude said slowly. "It would be just someone Father sent to pick it up for him."

"What *is* this?" Ed asked, in despair of both their intelligences. "Old man Graham has been dead for years."

Maude sighed and looked down at the dish towel which she had been twisting in her hands. Wister glanced at her and, seeing that her thoughts were turned inward, took the opportunity to slip away. He had come to the conclusion that he knew where Una was.

Ed was curious but he was also very hungry and he decided that his questions could wait until after he'd had lunch. He began to bustle around energetically, and Maude, coming out of her abstraction, threw the dish towel onto the floor and went on with the preparations for the meal. For a time they were both silent and then Ed began to get in the way so consistently that she asked in exasperation, "What's the matter with you, anyway? You ought to be able to do more around a kitchen than stumble over your feet and mine."

"God's sake," Ed said aggrievedly. "I've set the table and put the water on to boil."

"What are we boiling water for? Lobsters?"

"Lobsters would be nice," Ed murmured, and added hopefully, "Do you have any?"

"Oh, stop it, will you?" Maude exclaimed disgustedly. "Of course I have lobsters. I keep them in the bathtub but I haven't fed them lately, so maybe they're dead."

He grinned at her but she looked at the table on which he had arranged an assortment of cutlery and dishes and said, "Take the forks away, we shan't need them for boiled eggs."

Ed paled. "Maudie, listen, you don't really mean we're having boiled eggs for lunch?"

"That's right," she said firmly. " I can't afford to waste all this water you've boiled."

He gloomed in silence for a while but when at last they sat down, he saw that there were several tasty items in addition to the eggs and cheered up again.

"Where's Virginia?" Maude asked, pouring coffee.

"I dunno. I guess she went to work. She said she was going."

Maude took one of the boiled eggs, burned her fingers on the shell, and cursed quietly. Ed started to pour coffee, saw a pair of shoes appear on the floor beside the table, and looked up to find Viter standing beside him. A stream of coffee went over the edge of his cup and he demanded furiously, "Why can't you guys cough or something, if you have to pussyfoot around like an Indian in moccasins? I damn near had a heart attack and it would have been your fault."

Viter sat down at the table and addressed himself to Maude.

"Mrs. Watson, you must tell me the circumstances of your father's death."

Maude blushed, and Viter, knowing the reason, nevertheless took his mind off business long enough to admire it.

"There's not much to tell," Maude said, after a moment. "Father was away, down in Virginia, and he had a heart attack in the hotel. He died within a few hours."

"You heard from the local doctor?"

Maude nodded. "He asked for instructions and Bert went down to take care of things. I wanted him buried there because it never has seemed important to me where you bury people."

Ed looked a little shocked and Viter asked, "Didn't you or your sister go?"

"No, we didn't," Maude said defiantly. "Father was dead and we couldn't help him and we both hate funerals. Bert thought it was terrible, of course. He's always enjoyed a good funeral, and he was hardly speaking to us when he got back because we'd hurt his sense of propriety so badly. He wouldn't tell us anything about it for some long time but in the end he admitted he'd been too ashamed to go there and tell them the two daughters couldn't make the funeral because they had previous engagements. So he telephoned from another city and gave instructions over the phone."

"I see," Viter murmured gravely. "Yes. Now, I want you to come with me, Maude, while I see Dr. Bert and find out what he has to say."

It was the first time he had used her given name, and Maude was astounded to feel herself blushing again. She got up hastily and said, "All right, I ought to see him, anyway. I hear he had some sort of an accident."

They went across the street together. Mrs. Anderson admitted them to Bert's house. She didn't know too much about Bert's injury but she was able to give them the latest report on his mood.

"He just ain't fit to associate with a decent lady and gentleman like yourselves. Mr. Anderson says he's learned words he never knew before and he says I got to stick cotton in my ears if I keep on taking care of him."

Viter decided they'd chance it and see Bert anyway but he insisted that Maude stay out in the hall, just outside the door, while he went into the bedroom alone.

He found Bert trying to walk on the injured foot without much success. He had made the attempt because he could not stand lying in bed and thinking of Jim Larson attending to his pet patients. When Viter walked in and announced that he had a few questions to ask, Bert gave up and retired painfully to his bed.

"Can't you see I'm ill?" he whined. "I should think your questions could wait until a more propitious time."

"I'm sorry," Viter said courteously, "but the matter is pressing. I must know the details of the death of Oliver P. Graham."

"I don't know anything about it," Bert said irritably. "I stayed in an adjacent town, because I was ashamed at the girls not being there."

"And after it was all over," Viter said quietly, "did Mr. Graham turn up at your hotel?"

There was a dead silence and then Bert said simply, "Yes, he did. I don't know how he managed it but he turned up and wanted me to connive with him in getting the insurance money. Naturally I would have nothing to do with it and I have not seen him from that day to this."

"You have not seen him lately, masquerading around the town as P X. Smith?"

Bert turned his head on the pillow in a bothered way. "There was quite a resemblance, quite a resemblance, despite the goatee."

Viter nodded. "The funeral. Did no one attend?"

"Oh yes, yes. Plenty of people—friends and business acquaintances."

Viter considered for a moment. "Was it the sort of funeral where the corpse is on display for all to see?"

"Why, I suppose so," Bert said slowly. "I still wonder how he did it. He must have managed to get a cadaver that resembled him."

"Or perhaps," Viter said very distinctly, "the man who came around to your hotel resembled Oliver P. Graham." Bert was quiet for some time and then he nodded.

"Yes," he said, "I guess that was it."

CHAPTER 35

OUTSIDE BERT"S DOOR, Maude gave a little gasp, her hand reaching for the wall to steady herself. What was Bert saying? And how had Viter discovered these things? He was smooth, that one, smoother than she had realized.

Viter called to her and after a moment in which she tried to make her face carefully blank, she walked into the room. Bert raised his head from the pillow and she heard the sharp intake of his breath.

"Why were you standing outside the door, Maude?" he asked testily. "What a peculiar thing to do."

"I was taking a stone out of my shoe," she said promptly. "And anyway, how was I to know whether you had your nightshirt on or not? How are you feeling?"

"You can see how I'm feeling," Bert said bitterly. "Lying here ill and in pain, and no one caring whether I live or die."

"I know you're peevish, Bert," Maude said cheerfully. "That wasn't what I meant. I mean, how's the ankle feeling?"

Bert merely closed his eyes and Viter said with a half smile, "It's not too bad, I should think. When I came in, he was walking on it."

"Trying to walk on it, you mean," Bert declared in a fury. "I don't wish to sound rude but I am not in a fit state to entertain strangers. I'm afraid I must ask you to leave."

Viter said, "Sorry," and, slipping his arm through Maude's, steered her toward the door. Bert called after them that he'd like Maude to stay but either they did not hear him or they pretended not to and he was left alone.

In the downstairs hall they met Jim, coming in for another look at his patient, and Maude let out a small exclamation.

"You look like warmed-over ash, Jimmy. What's the matter?"

"Lack of sleep," he said briefly. "I didn't get any last night and today I've been rushing around handing out assorted pills to Hanson's patients as well as my own."

"What you need is some strong black coffee," Maude said firmly. "Come on back to the kitchen and I'll get it for you."

Jim glanced at his watch and said, "I haven't time," but Maude was already on her way to the kitchen and after a moment's hesitation he followed her.

"Have you had any lunch?" she called over her shoulder.

"No. Look, Maude—where's Virginia? She didn't go to work after all."

"Are you sure?" Viter asked sharply.

"Of course I'm sure. I dropped in to see her and they said she hadn't come in."

"Visiting her in office hours, yet," Maude said, looking interested. "Aloysius would have a stroke."

"Aloysius isn't supposed to know anything about it. I was doing it behind his back."

"Are you going to marry her over his dead body?" Maude asked.

"I mean, I think that's the only way it could be done."

Jim said a trifle austerely, "Aren't you being a little nosy?"

"Of course, it's a symptom of my age. Handing out advice is another compensation for middle age, so listen to me. You're just starting out as a doctor and I'm sponsoring you, which means that I can be as nosy as I like, and your only possible attitude is to answer politely, even while you bite your lips in vexation."

"Well, of course, if you put it that way," Jim agreed. "The situation is like this. I am not afraid of Aloysius because I have met up with bags of wind before. It's Virginia who bothers me. I have an idea that in the end she's going to turn me down."

"Oh, nonsense. You leave her to me. I'll talk to her."

Mrs. Anderson greeted them with pleasure and put on the coffee-pot at once. When she heard that Jim had had no sleep, nor, as yet, any lunch, she clicked her tongue in sympathy and set a full plate before him within the space of a few minutes.

Jim started in gratefully but when the first pangs had been satisfied he suspended his fork long enough to beg Maude not to interfere. He could handle Virginia himself and he would prefer to.

"Don't you be silly," Maude said emphatically. "There's nothing better than a good word put in, and I know just the word and where to put it in." She paused to laugh and added, "I'd like to see Wishy's face when he hears about it, though. It should rank with the seven wonders of the world."

Jim drained his coffee cup and Mrs. Anderson refilled it and then he asked, "What about Una?"

Maude's smile died away, and she sank back into her chair. "We haven't found her, and I don't know what to do."

"You should get the police in," Jim said, frowning. "It should have been done at once. I'd have done it myself if I hadn't been so busy. But I'll attend to it as soon as I've finished lunch."

"No need," Viter said quietly. "You're very busy. I shall do it myself."

"At once?" Jim demanded. "There shouldn't be any further delay."

"At once," said Viter, and walked purposefully out the back door.

As soon as he was out of sight of the kitchen windows, however, he slackened his pace and, apparently forgetting all about the police, he began to search the grounds of Bert's house. He was after some indication of where those two bodies had been hidden. He felt sure there were two of them, although he hadn't had the heart to tell Maude of his conviction that Una had been killed.

The man had been murdered, put in a temporary hiding place, and then removed. The woman had been killed in the museum and the same routine followed. But why all that extra trouble?

Viter concealed himself behind a forsythia bush and stretched out on the grass. He wanted to think without being interrupted. Smith, then, had been sleeping in the living room, and an intruder, ignorant of this fact, came in and switched on the light in the hall. He was after the money that the two women had been leaving in the attic, supposedly for their father, so he went straight up the stairs. P.X. Smith saw him go, thought it was a burglar, and followed.

In the meantime the bedside lamp in Aloysius's room had gone on in response to the hall switch but Aloysius, alternating between fear and fury, heard nothing of the intruder, nor of Smith following him. As a matter of fact, the intruder had been in several times, unconsciously turning Aloysius's lamp on each time, but he must have been quiet in his progress to the attic, since Aloysius had not once heard him. He had had his trouble for nothing, too, since the money was not there, Wister having taken it. Of course that bedside lamp had gone on once when Susan was in the room and the rest of them downstairs. But it could not have been the intruder that time. One of the group in the living room had turned the hall light on for something.

Viter folded his arms behind his head, closed his eyes, and thought over the plan of the Graham house. Ed could hear footsteps on the left wing staircase from his bedroom in the main part of the house but Aloysius was unable to hear them when he was right in the wing. Well, it was reasonable, after all. Ed's room was right next to the left wing staircase and Aloysius's room was actually some distance away.

Anyway, P.X. Smith followed the intruder up to the attic and the intruder, turning and seeing him suddenly, must have been drenched with horror. It would appear to be Oliver P.'s ghost, since he knew full well that Oliver P. was dead and buried. He smashed out at P.X. Smith in hysterical terror and the old man dropped without having uttered a sound. The intruder was still ignorant of the fact that the wing was occupied and he carried the body downstairs and sat it, temporarily, in the living room. He went out, desperately hunting for a place to hide it, and decided to bury it in the garden, so he came back and hauled it out. He cut the goatee off, still ghoulishly interested in the resemblance to Oliver P., and at last got the body buried.

But with Maude and Una always digging in the garden, it was a dangerous hiding place and he knew it. He wanted P.X. Smith simply to drop out of sight and never be seen again and so in the end he took him to a better hiding place.

That woman, Una, now—she had decided to light out of the place, so she went to the museum to get her suitcase. She lifted it off from the pile of luggage, set it on the floor and was murdered then and there. She was put into one of the old coffins temporarily, and Maude had walked in while she was still there.

Maude had noticed vaguely that the coffin lid was off, but her mind was on other things and it had not registered properly, which was lucky for the intruder, who was hiding in the museum at the time, waiting to remove the body. It was on that occasion that he had turned on the main electric switch for the wing in the basement so that he could see what he was doing. He had come in through the basement, no doubt. When he heard Maude approaching the museum, he'd turned the light off and hidden behind something while Una lay in that coffin with the lid off.

But Maude was so used to the museum that she hadn't looked about much and so she noticed nothing beyond the opened coffin lid and that more or less subconsciously. The intruder worked fast, after she had gone, hiding Una's body where P.X. Smith's was already hidden. He had wanted to get to her clothes and hide them, so that it would look as though she'd gone away, but he'd never had the chance.

Viter, feeling more or less satisfied with himself, chewed on a piece of grass and wondered idly where the scissors used to clip the goatee had come from.

A rumble of thunder cut across his thoughts and he realized that the sky was banked with coppery black clouds. As he looked up, lightning snaked through the dark mass and there was a louder crash of thunder. He got up and brushed himself off carefully, his mind still on the problem, and wondering now who would steal all that money and then put it in a cabinet in the museum. It seemed rather silly.

The first few drops of rain hurried him on his way, but he carried with him an impression of a face at one of the upper windows.

It was Virginia, but she had not noticed him. She had awakened to a dark room and lowering sky, and her first thought was that she had slept through till evening. She hurried to the window and realized that it was a summer storm instead. The room was hot and stuffy and she tried to open the window but it was stuck fast. She decided that she'd have to attract someone's attention and get herself released, even if Bert heard it and went into a tantrum.

She turned away from the window and in the semidarkness of the room pulled at a door and was surprised when it opened easily. She saw then that it was a closet door, instead of the one leading to the hall. The closet was long and narrow and she could see another door at the other end of it. She walked through, gave the farther door a tentative push and it opened into a bedroom. The furniture was shrouded in sheets and the blinds were drawn and when she tried the door leading to the hall, she found it locked firmly.

She hesitated, frowning and chewing nervously on her thumb, and then looked around quickly, saw a closet door at the side of the room, and hurried over to it. It opened without trouble, and she found the same arrangement here: a long narrow closet with another door at the far end. She walked through, stumbling a little over a dusty pile of old hatboxes, and pushed at the door. This one seemed to be stuck, but after several frantic heaves she was able to force it open. She glanced down and saw that the lock had been turned but had only partially caught and she shrugged as she realized that she had completed its disrepair.

This room was very dark, the furniture shrouded and the blinds drawn like the one behind her. As she stood trying to focus her eyes, there was a blinding flash of lightning, followed by a sharp clap of thunder and in the brief second when the room was flooded with light she saw that two bodies lay side by side on the bed.

CHAPTER 36

THE ONLY REMEMBRANCE that Virginia had later of that dreadful
moment in Bert's guest room was that she had started to faint and
then hadn't in the end because she thought Jim would sneer at her for
a sissy. She was never quite sure that this had actually been what
happened but it was the only memory she had of the moment. She
knew that she had quickly identified the bodies as Una and P.X.
Smith, although Smith was hardly recognizable. Certainly, without the
goatee, he did not look like Oliver P. Graham, since the mouth and
chin were different. The rest of the face was battered beyond human
semblance. Una's face had not been injured but it was evident that
she had been strangled.

Virginia backed away, flung herself against the door leading to the
hall and pounded frantically against the panels. There was a harsh,
sobbing sound coming from her throat but she did not know whether
she was laughing or crying. After a while she became vaguely conscious that someone was banging on the other side of the door and
shouting something and then, suddenly and quite easily, the door
opened.

Mrs. Anderson and Viter were outside, and she saw Viter remove a key from the lock and slip it into his pocket. A skeleton key,
Virginia thought. It must be a skeleton key and it had released her
from that dreadful room. She felt Mrs. Anderson's arms around her
and heard her murmur, "You poor lamb," before she hid her face on
the plump, comfortable shoulder.

Viter had gone into the room and Mrs. Anderson craned her neck
over Virginia's fair silken head but she could not see anything. Viter
presently emerged, looking grim, and closed the door firmly behind
him.

"Where's the telephone?" he asked abruptly.

"Down in the doctor's office," Mrs. Anderson whispered. "What's
happened? What is it?"

Virginia raised her head and drew a gasping breath. "I'll tell you.
I'll tell you all about it. But come downstairs. You mustn't look at it.
It's dreadful."

Viter, heading toward Bert's room, called over his shoulder, "Yes, you'd better go downstairs. And Mrs. Anderson, phone the police and tell them to come here at once."

"But what is it?" the bewildered woman asked. "You'd better let me see."

Viter stopped and turned toward her. "No. Go down and phone the police."

Mrs. Anderson went, her arm still supporting Virginia and her forehead pulled into a puzzled frown.

Viter went straight to Bert's room and stopped abruptly just inside the door. Bert was not there.

He must be hiding, Viter thought. He must have heard all the uproar. But with that ankle he couldn't go very fast or very far.

Viter started a swift, systematic search, opening doors, looking under beds, and occasionally muttering to himself. Bert, he thought, was just the type to carry a pair of scissors around with him—probably a needle and thread too, in case he lost a button. Also, he knew that Oliver P. Graham was dead, that was obvious. Saying that Oliver P. had turned up at his hotel after the funeral and then agreeing in the next breath that it could have been an impostor. Further, he had declared that there were a lot of friends, business and social, at the funeral and that the corpse had been on display. It was nonsense to suppose that that corpse could have been anyone but Oliver P. because had it been anyone else, someone would certainly have spotted it. Yet Bert had allowed Maude and Una to think that their father was still alive.

Maude had gone home just before the storm and was crouched in a chair in her bedroom. She was afraid of thunderstorms and so ashamed of her fear that she tried to keep it a secret. She was alone in the house, and she wished, uneasily, that Aloysius and Ed had not gone into town. Even Wister, she remembered, had gone off somewhere, looking for Una, probably. The expression on his face had indicated to Maude that he thought he knew where Una was, and of course he was all wrong. No doubt he supposed that she had gone to one of his relatives to prepare for her marriage to him, and it was silly of Wister to think that Una would bother with anything of the sort.

A white sheet of lightning flashed into the room, followed by a tremendous crash of thunder. Maude cowered back and closed her eyes and the thought of Bert slid into her mind.

He had told Una and herself that their father's funeral had been absolutely private, with no one there. And yet today he had told Viter that a great many people had attended. Bert didn't tell lies, as a rule, either. He didn't believe in them. He had always been truthful in small things. Yet she remembered that she and Una had caught him in one or two heavy lies over the course of the years, but only when there was something big too be gained by it or some prestige to be gained for himself.

But this news about the funeral meant that Father had been dead all the time, and Maude wrinkled her forehead as she thought back to the telephone call and the letter from Father after the funeral. Only, of course, they must both have come from Bert, who wanted them to believe that Father was still alive. Bert had done it all, the whole thing. And he knew that she'd heard his remark about the funeral and that she'd figure it out from there.

Maude glanced uneasily at the door. Bert couldn't come after her with his ankle in that state, surely he couldn't. But Viter had said he'd been walking on it, so perhaps he could. She shivered and glanced at the telephone. She'd call the police the instant the storm let up but she was afraid to use the telephone with a thunderstorm raging outside. Silly, but she couldn't help it.

But would Bert have harmed Una? Of course he was furious about the broken engagement. She remembered his dark, set face when she had told him about it, and almost immediately he had stalked out to make the cocktails. He was fussy in everything he did but she remembered thinking that he had taken rather a long time over those cocktails.

Maude became conscious of a sick feeling in the pit of her stomach. Bert hadn't been mixing drinks all that time. Probably they'd been mixed and ready before she arrived.

He must have come straight over to the house and caught Una in the museum and killed her in a fury. Bert was like that. He'd worked for years to marry one of them in order to gain prestige for himself and actually he didn't even like either of them. So he had indulged his frustration and fury in the end and killed Una.

Maude started out of her chair with her breath coming in sick gasps. She'd go and get the whole story out of Bert, and he'd pay for it. The lightning flashed again and she sank back. She did not have to go after Bert, anyway. He'd come after her. If there were any way that he could get here with his injured ankle, he'd make it, because he'd have to stop her mouth now, too. He knew that she'd have it figured out by now.

He could afford to go on indulging his fury, at this point. He'd killed twice already and one more didn't matter.

She thought of the money and shook her head a little. Bert hadn't done it for the money. He loved money, but it had to be his own, and he wouldn't have taken theirs. That's why he had hidden it around the house, so that he could tell himself that he had not stolen it. But he hadn't wanted them to have any money, he wanted them down, away down so that he could lord it over them. Years ago it had eaten into his soul like an acid to see Maude and Una throwing money around on luxuries when he himself had none. Of course Bert would never have thrown money around, no matter how much he might have had, but it had always been a bitter thing for him to see other people doing it. Maude gave a giggle that ended on a cracked sound and then sternly told herself to stop it.

Yes, Bert would come after her, no matter how much his ankle pained him. When he made up his mind to a thing, his determination was inflexible. He'd come. And what better time could there be than during a heavy thunderstorm in the afternoon? Mrs. Anderson usually took a nap during the afternoon, too. Maude held her rocking chair still and listened.

Why, he was all the way up the stairs already. He was limping badly and his breath was loud and labored as he came down the long hall toward her room.

CHAPTER 37

MAUDE GOT SLOWLY to her feet, her eyes on the dim outline of the door. She'd have to do something quickly because he was coming to kill her, like P.X. Smith. No, he wouldn't batter her face to a pulp. He'd do it some other way, something faster and more efficient.

A belated urge to lock the door sent her halfway across the room but she was too late. Bert limped in, his face grim with lines of pain, and closed the door behind him. Maude saw the revolver in his hand and froze where she stood.

"Back up, Maude," he said jerkily. "This is the end for you. I've put up with your high-stepping, arrogant family for long enough. I never want to see another sneering Graham face."

Maude backed up, her eyes fastened to the revolver. "What did I ever do to you, Bert?" she asked quietly.

"What did you ever do to me?" he repeated shrilly. "You and all your tribe, laughing and carrying on, throwing money to the four winds, while I crawled through college, wondering where the next meal was coming from. I made a success of my profession and still you had more money than I did. And threw it in my face. And you wouldn't marry me, either one of you. I wasn't good enough. But I fixed you for a while, didn't I? I had you and that nasty sister of yours wondering how you were going to keep your proud faces fed.

"And then, last night, Una thought old Oliver was dead at last, so she kicked me away without a second thought. She'd been willing to marry me, at last, simply for the money she could get out of it and when she thought it wasn't necessary any longer, she hadn't even the decency to come and tell me herself. I found her there in the museum and I strangled her with my bare hands."

Maude shuddered and whispered, "Bert, you're lying."

"I'm not lying. I'm going to send you after her. I didn't know you were outside the door when I told that detective that your father's funeral had been well attended and then, when you walked in, I knew it wouldn't take you long to figure it out. Here, Maude."

Lightning flashed vividly into the room and at the same time the shot rang out. But the lightning had distracted Bert and the bullet went wild. Maude dropped to the floor at once and scrambled under the bed. Bert, after a dazed look at the revolver in his hand, began a slow, painful advance. He'd have to lean down and shoot under the bed, and then he must wipe the revolver carefully and leave it with her. No one would connect it with him, since it had belonged to old Oliver P.

If only the pain in his ankle were not so bad. It was like a thousand red-hot needles. But he must get this thing done. He rested one hand on the edge of the bed and started to bend down, and suddenly the small mat on which he stood was jerked sharply, and he stumbled, lost his balance, and fell.

His ankle seemed to go off like a series of skyrockets and he sank back into a dark river of pain. He knew that he must rouse himself, that if Maude ever got out of the room, it was the end of him. He dragged his heavy eyes open to see her disappearing out of the door. Even then he tried to send a shot after her, but he could not raise his leaden arm from the floor. The drugs had betrayed him in the end. He had taken too much in his effort to ease the pain. It didn't matter. It was all over and he would wake up in prison. He closed his eyes and let the dark river wash over him.

When he awoke, he was not in prison, but in Maude's bed. The room seemed to be filled with people, all talking and making noise, while he lay there, neglected and in pain. Ed Randall was there, talking loudly as he always did. And why should Una have married a tricky, vulgar person like that and scorned Bert, who was dependable and honest? Yes, he had been honest, always, until they goaded him into this last outburst.

"But I don't get it," Ed was saying. "I still don't see how footsteps could go halfway up the stairs and then stop."

Bert moved his head restlessly. No, Ed wouldn't get it, because he hadn't a brain in his head, and yet Una had married him. As for the footsteps going halfway up the stairs, it was simple enough. He'd been walking up on his way to the attic to look for P.X. Smith's missing slipper and his shoes had sounded so loud on the stairs that, halfway up, he'd taken them off and gone on in his socks. He'd known by that time that there were people staying in the left wing and he'd had to be a lot more careful about making any noise.

Poor old Smith had been an innocent victim because of his resemblance to Oliver P. The odd part of it was that when Bert had cut off the goatee, in a moment of superstitious fear, the resemblance was not nearly so marked. The mouth and chin were quite different. Burying Smith in the garden had been pure panic, but later he'd removed him to the guest room, along with all his belongings, so that it would look as though he had simply departed. It would have worked that way, too, but for Aloysius blundering into the living room. Bert shivered. He hadn't known about all those people being in the left wing, and he'd gone around turning lights on and making no particular effort to be quiet.

Ed was still talking, and Bert heard him say, "But you couldn't kill an old man like that without making any noise."

Oh, couldn't you, though. Bert felt moisture on his forehead as he thought back to the horror of that moment. He'd been looking for the money in that ghostly attic and it wasn't there. Then he turned and thought he saw the face of old Oliver P. in the faint light of the stairwell. Almost at once he realized that it was the man he had seen in the restaurant and he thought that he'd been followed and was about to be blackmailed. In a frenzy of fear, he threw his gun. It caught Smith on the side of the head. He dropped without a sound and Bert, completely berserk for a few minutes, pounded madly at the face and head with the butt of the gun.

He thought of Una and of his strong hands on her soft neck while Maude sat waiting for cocktails. Being jilted by Una was the final humiliation. Killing her had made him feel superior and strong. She lay in that old coffin in the museum while he and Maude drank their cocktails and ate dinner. Later he'd brought her to his house and put her in the guest room with P.X. Smith.

It had been a bad moment when Maude had walked into the museum and put the light on. He had cursed himself, then, for throwing the main switch in the cellar on his way in, but he had thought he might need some light. He'd crouched down behind the coffins expecting every moment to be discovered and then Maude had gone out again and it was all right.

Aloysius was arguing loudly with Ed. "You're all wrong. Listen to me, will you? Wister went over and searched Bert's house for the money but he couldn't find it because it wasn't there. He knew Bert was taking it and he wanted to find out if he was spending any of it on Una. Only he wasn't, of course. He was putting it in places like that Chinese cabinet. He took it out of the cabinet when he heard that we were searching the house, because, of course, he didn't want it to be discovered. Thought it might point in his direction, and he was right. It was an asinine thing to do, and Bert's a donkey."

Yes, Bert thought bitterly, because he was honest, they called him a donkey. He had never used anybody's money but his own.

Viter and Maude were murmuring intimately together. What did Viter have in the way of culture, education, and prestige that Maude should bat her eyes at him when she had merely laughed at Bert from his childhood on?

Larson was hanging over Aloysius's girl, another Graham, and she was undoubtedly giving him a dewy-eyed look. Who was Larson, a young and inexperienced fool, that one of the Grahams should pass the time of day with him?

Aloysius turned suddenly, caught the dewy-eyed look himself, and yelled, "For God's, sake, Ginny, do you have to sit with that ape? If you've got to be that close to him, can't you spit in his eye, or something?"

Jim stood up and faced Aloysius squarely. "Mr. Graham, may I have your daughter's hand?"

"No!" Aloysius roared. "She needs it herself."

Maude, disturbed by the noise, turned away from Viter, although she carelessly left her hand clasped in his. "You shut up, Wishy. This is a good way to end the Graham-Larson feud forever. If you Grahams don't agree to the marriage, you can start house hunting again as of now."

Aloysius, who had drawn in a breath to blast her with a vociferous reply, let it out again, slowly and silently, and appeared to sag in all his joints.

Virginia sighed. "Anything," she said distinctly, "even Jim Larson, is better than being homeless."

THE END

About The Rue Morgue Press

The Rue Morgue vintage mystery line is designed to bring back into print those books that were favorites of readers between the turn of the century and the 1960s. The editors welcome suggests for reprints. To receive our catalog or make suggestions, write The Rue Morgue Press, P.O. Box 4119, Boulder, Colorado (1-800-699-6214).

Catalog of Rue Morgue Press titles
as of February 2004

Titles are listed by author. All books are quality trade paperbacks measuring 9 by 6 inches, usually with full-color covers and printed on paper designed not to yellow or deteriorate. These are permanent books.

Joanna Cannan. The books by this English writer are among our most popular titles. Modern reviewers favorably compared our two Cannan reprints with the best books of the Golden Age of detective fiction. "Worthy of being discussed in the same breath with an Agatha Christie or a Josephine Tey."—Sally Fellows, *Mystery News.* "First-rate Golden Age detection with a likeable detective, a complex and believable murderer, and a level of style and craft that bears comparison with Sayers, Allingham, and Marsh."—Jon L. Breen, *Ellery Queen's Mystery Magazine.* Set in the late 1930s in a village that was a fictionalized version of Oxfordshire, both titles feature young Scotland Yard inspector Guy Northeast. *They Rang Up the Police* (0-915230-27-5, $14.00) and *Death at The Dog* (0-915230-23-2, $14.00).

Glyn Carr. The author is really Showell Styles, one of the foremost English mountain climbers of his era as well as one of that sport's most celebrated historians. Carr turned to crime fiction when he realized that mountains provided a ideal setting for committing murders. The 15 books featuring Shakespearean actor Abercrombie "Filthy" Lewker are set on peaks scattered around the globe, although the author returned again and again to his favorite climbs in Wales, where his first mystery, published in 1951, *Death on Milestone Buttress* (0-915230-29-1, $14.00), is set. Lewker is a marvelous Falstaffian character whose exploits have been praised by such discerning critics as Jacques Barzun and Wendell Hertig Taylor in *A Catalogue of Crime.*

Torrey Chanslor. *Our First Murder* (0-915230-50-X, $14.95). When a headless corpse is discovered in a Manhattan theatrical lodging house, who better to call in than the Beagle sisters? Sixty-five-year-old Amanda employs good old East Biddicut common sense to run the agency, while her younger sister Lutie prowls the streets and nightclubs of 1940 Manhattan looking for clues. It's their first murder case since inheriting the Beagle Private Detective Agency from their older brother, but you'd never know the sisters had spent all of their lives knitting and tending to their garden in a small, sleepy upstate New York town. Lutie is a real charmer, who learned her craft by reading scores of lurid detective novels borrowed from the East Biddicut Circulating Library. With her younger cousin Marthy in tow, Lutie is totally at ease as she questions suspects and orders vintage champagne. Of course, if trouble pops up, there's always that pearl-handled revolver tucked away in her purse. *Our First Murder* is a charming hybrid of the private eye, traditional, and cozy mystery, written in 1940 by a woman who earned two Caldecott nominations for her illustrations of children's books. *Our Second Murder* (0-915230-64-X, $14.95) will be published early in 2004. The sisters look into the murder of a socialite who was strangled with a diamond necklace. Final book in series.

Clyde B. Clason. Clason has been praised not only for his elaborate plots and skillful use of the locked room gambit but also for his scholarship. He may be one of the few mystery authors—and no doubt the first—to provide a full bibliography of his sources. *The Man from Tibet* (0-915230-17-8, $14.00) is one of his best (selected in 2001 in *The History of Mystery* as one of the 25 great amateur detective novels of all time) and highly recommended by the dean of locked room mystery scholars, Robert Adey, as "highly original." It's also one of the first popular novels to make use of Tibetan culture. *Murder Gone Minoan* (0-915230-60-7, $14.95) is set on a channel island off the coast of Southern California where a Greek department store magnate has recreated a Minoan palace.

Joan Coggin. *Who Killed the Curate?* Meet Lady Lupin Lorrimer Hastings, the young, lovely, scatterbrained and kindhearted daughter of an earl, now the newlywed wife of the vicar of St. Marks Parish in Glanville, Sussex. When it comes to matters clerical, she literally doesn't know Jews from Jesuits and she's hopelessly at sea at meetings of the Mothers' Union, Girl Guides, or Temperance Society, but she's determined to make husband Andrew proud of her—or, at least, not to embarrass him too badly. So when Andrew's curate is poisoned, Lady Lupin enlists the help of her old society pals, Duds and Tommy Lethbridge, as well as Andrew's nephew, a British secret service agent, to get at the truth. Lupin refuses to believe Diana Lloyd, the 38-year-old author of children's and detective stories, could have done the deed, and casts her net out over the other parishioners. All the suspects seem so nice, much more so than the victim, and Lupin announces she'll help the killer escape if only he or she confesses. Set at Christmas 1937 and first published in England in 1944, this is the first American appearance of *Who Killed the Curate?* "Marvelous."—*Deadly Pleasures*. "A complete delight."—*Reviewing the Evidence*. (0-915230-44-5, $14.00). The comic antics continue unabated in *The Mystery at Orchard House* (0-915230-54-2, $14.95), *Penelope Passes or Why Did She Die?* (0-915230-61-5, $14.95), and *Dancing with Death* (0-915230-62-3, $14.95), the fourth and final book in the series.

Manning Coles. The two English writers who collaborated as Coles are best known for those witty spy novels featuring Tommy Hambledon, but they also wrote four delightful—and funny—ghost novels. *The Far Traveller* (0-915230-35-6, $14.00) is a stand-alone novel in which a film company unknowingly hires the ghost of a long-dead German graf to play himself in a movie. "I laughed until I hurt. I liked it so much, I went back to page 1 and read it a second time."—Peggy Itzen, *Cozies, Capers & Crimes*. The other three books feature two cousins, one English, one American, and their spectral pet monkey who got a little drunk and tried to stop—futilely and fatally—a German advance outside a small French village during the 1870 Franco-Prussian War. Flash forward to the 1950s where this comic trio of friendly ghosts rematerialize to aid relatives in danger in *Brief Candles* (0-915230-24-0, 156 pages, $14.00), *Happy Returns* (0-915230-31-3, $14.00) and *Come and Go* (0-915230-34-8, $14.00).

Norbert Davis. There have been a lot of dogs in mystery fiction, from Baynard Kendrick's guide dog to Virginia Lanier's bloodhounds, but there's never been one quite like Carstairs. Doan, a short, chubby Los Angeles private eye, won Carstairs in a crap game, but there never is any question as to who the boss is in this relationship. Carstairs isn't just any Great Dane. He is so big that Doan figures he really ought to be considered another species. He scorns baby talk and belly rubs—unless administered by a pretty girl—and growls whenever Doan has a drink. His full name is Dougal's Laird Carstairs and as a sleuth he rarely barks up the wrong tree. He's down in Mexico with Doan, ostensibly to convince a missing fugitive that he would do well to stay put, in *The Mouse in the Mountain* (0-915230-41-0, $14.00), first published in 1943 and followed by two other Doan and Carstairs novels. A staff pick at The Sleuth of Baker Street in Toronto, Murder by the Book in Houston and The Poisoned Pen in Scottsdale. Four star review in *Romantic Times*. "A laugh a minute romp…hilarious dialogue and descriptions…utterly engaging, downright fun read…fetch this one! Highly recommended."—Michele A. Reed, *I Love a Mystery*. "Deft, charming…unique…one of my top ten all time favorite novels."—Ed Gorman, *Mystery Scene*. The second book, *Sally's in the Alley* (0-915230-46-1, $14.00), was equally well-received. *Publishers Weekly*: "Norbert Davis committed suicide in 1949, but his incomparable crime-fighting duo, Doan, the tippling private eye, and Carstairs, the huge and preternaturally clever Great Dane, march on in a re-release of the 1943 *Sally's in the Alley*. Doan's on a government-sponsored mission to find an ore deposit in the Mojave Desert…in an old-fashioned romp that matches its bloody crimes with belly laughs." The editor of *Mystery Scene* chimed in: "I love Craig Rice. Davis is her equal." "The funniest P.I. novel ever written."—*The Drood Review*. The raves continued for final book in the trilogy, *Oh, Murderer Mine* (0-915230-57-7, $14.00). "He touches the hardboiled markers but manages to run amok in a genre known for confinement. . .This book is just plain funny."—Ed Lin, *Forbes.com*.

Elizabeth Dean. In Emma Marsh Dean created one of the first independent female sleuths in the genre. Written in the screwball style of the 1930s, the Marsh books were described in a review in *Deadly Pleasures* by award-winning mystery writer Sujata Massey as a series that "froths over with the same effervescent humor as the best Hepburn-Grant films." *Murder is a Serious Business* (0-915230-28-3, $14.95), is set in a Boston antique store just as the Great Depression is drawing to a close. *Murder a Mile High* (0-915230-39-9, $14.00) moves to the Central City Opera House in the Colorado mountains, where Emma has been summoned by an old chum, the opera's reigning diva. Emma not only has to find a murderer, she may also have to catch a Nazi spy. "Fascinating."—*Romantic Times.*

Constance & Gwenyth Little. These two Australian-born sisters from New Jersey have developed almost a cult following among mystery readers. Critic Diane Plumley, writing in *Dastardly Deeds*, called their 21 mysteries "celluloid comedy written on paper." Each book, published between 1938 and 1953, was a stand-alone, but there was no mistaking a Little heroine. She hated house-work, wasn't averse to a little gold-digging (so long as she called the shots), and couldn't help antagonizing cops and potential beaux. The result is one of the oddest mixtures in all of crime fiction. It's what might happen if P.G. Wodehouse and Cornell Woolrich had collaborated on a crime novel. The Rue Morgue Press intends to reprint all of their books. Currently available are: *The Black Thumb* (0-915230-48-8, $14.00), *The Black Coat* (0-915230-40-2, $14.00), *Black Corridors* (0-915230-33-X, $14.00), *The Black Gloves* (0-915230-20-8, $14.00), *Black-Headed Pins* (0-915230-25-9, $14.00), *The Black Honeymoon* (0-915230-21-6, $14.00), *The Black Paw* (0-915230-37-2, $14.00), *The Black Stocking* (0-915230-30-5, $14.00), *Great Black Kanba* (0-915230-22-4, $14.00), *The Grey Mist Murders* (0-915230-26-7, $14.00), *The Black Eye* (0-915230-45-3, $14.00), *The Black Shrouds* (0-915230-52-6, $14.00), *The Black Rustle* (0-915230-58-5, $14.00) and *The Black Goatee* (0-915230-63-1, $14.00). *The Black Piano* (0-915230-65-8) is due to be published in March 2004.

Marlys Millhiser. Our only non-vintage mystery, *The Mirror* (0-915230-15-1, $17.95) is our all-time bestselling book, now in a seventh printing. How could you not be intrigued by a novel in which "you find the main character marrying her own grandfather and giving birth to her own mother," as one reviewer put it of this supernatural, time-travel (sort of) piece of wonderful make-believe set both in the mountains above Boulder, Colorado, at the turn of the century and in the city itself in 1978. Internet book services list scores of rave reviews from readers who often call it the "best book I've ever read."

James Norman. The marvelously titled *Murder, Chop Chop* (0-915230-16-X, $13.00) is a wonderful example of the eccentric detective novel. "The book has the butter-wouldn't-melt-in-his-mouth cool of Rick in *Casablanca*."—*The Rocky Mountain News*. "Amuses the reader no end."—*Mystery News*. "This long out-of-print masterpiece is intricately plotted, full of eccentric characters and very humorous indeed. Highly recommended."—*Mysteries by Mail*. Meet Gimiendo Hernandez Quinto, a gigantic Mexican who once rode with Pancho

Villa and who now trains *guerrilleros* for the Nationalist Chinese government when he isn't solving murders. At his side is a beautiful Eurasian known as Mountain of Virtue, a woman as dangerous to men as she is irresistible. First published in 1942.

Sheila Pim. *Ellery Queen's Mystery Magazine* said of these wonderful Irish village mysteries that Pim "depicts with style and humor everyday life." *Booklist* said they were in "the best tradition of Agatha Christie." Beekeeper Edward Gildea uses his knowledge of bees and plants to good use in *A Hive of Suspects* (0-915230-38-0, $14.00). *Creeping Venom* (0-915230-42-9, $14.00) blends politics and religion into a deadly mixture. *A Brush with Death* (0-915230-49-6, $14.00) grafts a clever art scam onto the stem of a gardening mystery.

Craig Rice. *Home Sweet Homicide.* This marvelously funny and utterly charming tale (set in 1942 and first published in 1944) of three children who "help" their widowed mystery writer mother solve a real-life murder and nab a handsome cop boyfriend along the way made just about every list of the best mysteries for the first half of the 20th century, including the Haycraft-Queen Cornerstone list (probably the most prestigious honor roll in the history of crime fiction), James Sandoe's *Reader's Guide to Crime,* and Melvyn Barnes' *Murder in Print.* Rice was of course best known for her screwball mystery comedies featuring Chicago criminal attorney John J. Malone. *Home Sweet Homicide* is a delightful cozy mystery partially based on Rice's own home life. Rice, the first mystery writer to appear on the cover of *Time*, died in 1957 at the age of 49 (0-915230-53-4, $14.95).

Charlotte Murray Russell. Spinster sleuth Jane Amanda Edwards tangles with a murderer and Nazi spies in *The Message of the Mute Dog* (0-915230-43-7, $14.00), a culinary cozy set just before Pearl Harbor. "Perhaps the mother of today's cozy."—*The Mystery Reader.*

Sarsfield, Maureen. These two mysteries featuring Inspector Lane Parry of Scotland Yard are among our most popular books. Both are set in Sussex. *Murder at Shots Hall* (0-915230-55-8, $14.95) features Flikka Ashley, a thirtyish sculptor with a past she would prefer remain hidden. It was originally published as *Green December Fills the Graveyard* in 1945. Parry is back in Sussex, trapped by a blizzard at a country hotel where a war hero has been pushed out of a window to his death in *Murder at Beechlands* (0-915230-56-9, $14.95). First published in 1948 in England as *A Party for None* and in the U.S. as *A Party for Lawty.* The owner of Houston's Murder by the Book called these two books the best publications from The Rue Morgue Press.

Juanita Sheridan. Sheridan was one of the most colorful figures in the history of detective fiction, as you can see from the introduction to *The Chinese Chop* (0-915230-32-1, 155 pages, $14.00). Her books are equally colorful, as well as examples of how mysteries with female protagonists began changing after World War II. The postwar housing crunch finds Janice Cameron, newly arrived in New York City from Hawaii, without a place to live until she answers an ad for a roommate. It turns out the advertiser is an acquaintance from Hawaii, Lily Wu. First published in 1949, this ground-breaking book was the first of four to feature Lily and be told by her Watson, Janice, a first-time novelist. "Highly recommended."—*I Love a Mystery*. "Puts to lie the common misconception that strong, self-reliant, non-spinster-or-comic sleuths didn't appear on the scene until the 1970s."—*Ellery Queen's Mystery Magazine*. The first book in the series to be set in Hawaii is *The Kahuna Killer* (0-915230-47-X, $14.00). "Originally published five decades ago (though it doesn't feel like it), this detective story featuring charming Chinese sleuth Lily Wu has the friends and foster sisters investigating mysterious events—blood on an ancient altar, pagan rites, and the appearance of a kahuna (a witch doctor)—and the death of a sultry hula girl in 1950s Oahu."—*Publishers Weekly*. Third in the series is *The Mamo Murders* (0915230-51-8, $14.00), set on a Maui cattle ranch. The final book in the quartet, *The Waikiki Widow* (0-915230-59-3, $14.00) is set in Honolulu tea industry.